CODENAME ZERO

CHRIS RYLANDER

CODE ZERO

WALDEN POND PRESS
An Imprint of HarperCollins*Publishers*

Walden Pond Press is an imprint of HarperCollins Publishers.
Walden Pond Press and the skipping stone logo are trademarks and registered
trademarks of Walden Media, LLC.

Codename: Zero

Library of Congress Cataloging-in-Publication Data
Rylander, Chris.
  Codename: Zero / Chris Rylander.
    pages cm
  Summary: "When a desperate man in a nondescript black suit asks thirteen-year-
old Carson Fender to deliver a mysterious package for him, the middle schooler
discovers there's something going on in his sleepy North Dakota hometown he had
never expected"— Provided by publisher.
  ISBN 978-0-06-212008-3 (hardback) — ISBN 978-0-06-232530-3 (int'l ed.)
  [1. Adventure and adventurers—Fiction. 2. Spies—Fiction. 3. Middle schools—
Fiction. 4. Schools—Fiction. 5. Humorous stories.] I. Title.
PZ7.R98147Cod 2014   2013032327
[Fic]—dc23   CIP
                                                                           AC

Typography by Michelle Gengaro-Kokmen
13 14 15 16 17 CG/RRDH 10 9 8 7 6 5 4 3 2 1
❖
First Edition

For Mom and Dad

CODENAME
ZER⭕

CHAPTER 1

THERE I WAS IN THE PARKING LOT OF MY SCHOOL, MINDING my own business, when some mysterious dude shows up and hands me an even more mysterious package. Okay, so I wasn't so much minding my own business as I was putting the finishing touches on the fourth biggest prank in Erik Hill Middle School history. But the point was the same—I was busy. I didn't really have time to talk to this guy who'd just run up to me as if he were in the middle of a race with his own shadow. Sweat poured down his face and he was breathing so hard I thought he was going to literally cough up a chunk of his lung onto one of my brand-new sneakers.

The sweating and panting itself wasn't all that strange—I mean, lots of weirdos like to go for runs. But just not usually in a black business suit and tie at 2:55 in the afternoon on a 100-degree day with a sun so blazing that lizards were melting on sidewalks all over town. At least his black sunglasses actually fit the sunny situation.

"Hey, kid," the guy said.

I tried to ignore him, because like I said, I was busy. But he was persistent.

"Hey!" he said again, frantically grabbing my arm.

"What?" I asked.

"Take this."

Suddenly I was holding a package. It was about the size of a shoe box but only half as thick. And it was wrapped in plain brown paper with no markings of any kind on it and clear tape holding the folds in place. The wrapping was tight and neat, the same way my mom likes to basically suffocate Christmas presents when she wraps them. It was clean, too, except for the damp spots where his sweaty fingers had touched it.

My first thought was that someone was playing a prank on me. I should know; I'd done my share of them over the years. In fact, counting the one I was about to execute, I would now be responsible for the all-time top five pranks in school history. But there was something about the guy's desperate and almost terrified look that kept me from laughing at him and handing the package back.

"What am I supposed to . . . ?"

"Just listen," he said, while glancing over both shoulders quickly. "You must guard this with your life; the fate of the world depends on it. And whatever you do, don't open it!"

"What?"

He flipped a finger under the lens of his sunglasses and wiped away a stream of sweat. "You must deliver this to Mr. Jensen. It must go *only* to Mr. Jensen, you understand? Trust no one."

He didn't get a chance to say anything more because at that moment the school bell rang. Our school still had a bell on the outside of it that rang every day at 3:00 when school was out. And on this particular day, it also signaled my friend, Dillon, to initiate the first phase of the prank. So when the bell rang, chaos broke out.

I turned back to the guy to ask him again what I was supposed to do with the package, but he was no longer there. He was running away from me, across the parking lot toward Sixteenth Street. He ran right by the stream of goats that was headed toward the school's front entrance. And now two guys with painted white faces were chasing him.

I didn't have time to wonder who he was, where he was going, or where the guys with the white faces had come from. Because shortly after the bell rang, kids started filing out of the school. That was my cue to get the heck out of there.

Also, that's when the herd of fainting goats reached the front entrance of the school.

If you've never seen a fainting goat in action, you're missing out. They're one of the few things in North Dakota worth seeing. Basically it's this breed of goat that faints when they get scared. And they serve no other practical purpose, even to a farmer, which in my book makes them about the most perfect animal in the world. All they do is eat grass and faint.

But today they had an actual purpose. Or several. For one, hundreds of goats running and fainting all over a school lawn at 3:00 was just plain hilarious to see, especially when your school's mascot is Gordy, the Fighting Billy Goat. But more important, the chaos they'd create would provide a big enough distraction for me to execute the real prank. One that involved something very simple: glue.

That's right, glue. I mean, gluing a teacher's computer mouse to their desk was a classic. Nothing new there, I get it. But what about if it were taken to a new, ridiculous level? Such as supergluing every single door in the school shut? Including the principal's? And that would be only after gluing down all the items on his desk, of course. Plus we'd glue all the items on all the other teachers' desks. And all the lockers in the locker room, all the science supplies in the storeroom, all the mops and brooms in the maintenance closets, everything. Basically the whole school would be on Glue-Down. Incapacitated when the day started tomorrow. That's what made the goats so purposeful today. Simply pulling the fire alarm wouldn't work since teachers had to then make sure that all kids exited the building before they did. But a whole herd of fainting goats? Well, for that, the school would simply empty altogether in an attempt to control the situation with no regard for who snuck back in or stayed behind to do whatever their hearts desired.

So, basically, it was pandemonium . . . or goatemonium is probably a better word for it. There were goats running and yelling, kids running and yelling, and then the goats started fainting. Teachers started coming outside to see what the commotion was, which led to more yelling and goats fainting. I even saw one goat chewing on a teacher's pant leg right before it fainted, the pants still clutched in its jaws as it went rigid and fell over.

Everything was going exactly as planned. My best friends, Dillon and Danielle, and our usual accomplices, Zack and Ethan, were probably already splitting up into the various areas of the school, gluing stuff down wherever they found it. And I should have been inside already, too, helping them with Principal Gomez's office before he got suspicious and headed back inside the school himself.

But I wasn't inside gluing.

All because of the sweaty guy in the suit. I was still standing there, mostly watching the pale-faced guys chase the sweaty dude in the black suit. Right at the corner of Sixteenth and Burdick the two pasty weirdos caught him. One tackled him right onto the pavement. And I saw, even as kids laughed and screamed and goats were fainting all around me, their legs sticking straight up in the air like upside-down tables, that a black sedan had stopped next to the three men. Another guy in a suit jumped out and helped the pasty dudes shove the former package bearer inside the car.

That's also when I saw the guns in their hands.

And one of them looked right at me before he got into the car. I could have sworn, even at that distance and even among the fainting, petrified goats and screaming kids and parents honking their car horns and teachers trying to calm everyone down, that he saw me holding the package. But then they all piled into the car and it sped off and I was left there, holding this thing and staring right at the principal, who had come out of nowhere.

Mr. Gomez scowled at me in that way that only principals can.

"Mr. Fender. My office. Right now."

100101101010100000101010010101010100100000
0101010010010010101010010101001010101001010
010100001001010010101010010101010101010101
000101010101010100110010101010101010101010
01010101010100000101001010101001010101010
0101000010010100101010100101010101010101
00001   00110010101010101010101010
001   00101010100101010100101010100
1   10101001010101010101010

CHAPTER 2

AS I FOLLOWED MR. GOMEZ IN THE DIRECTION OF HIS OFFICE
I could only hope that my friends were either finished
gluing in there or would see us through the office window before it was too late. The plan was to rendezvous at
Gomez's office just a few minutes after the goats were let
out, to make sure we got his office done first.

I know it may seem like a lot for a prank—gathering
up a whole herd of goats and orchestrating their release
onto the front lawn just as the school bell rang—and all
so my friends and I could coat the school in glue. Isn't that

a long way to go for a few laughs? Sure, I guess it is. But at the same time, what's the alternative? Another boring small-town North Dakota day, that's what. Another day riding the bus to school, watching kids who pretty much all look and act and dress the same, talking about the same stuff they did the day before, going to and from their classes all so they can finish middle school, go to the same high school, go to one of the two large state universities, just so they can end up right back here in town working the same boring jobs as their parents, and then have kids of their own and start the whole thing all over again.

It's the same routine people here had been following for generations. *That* was the alternative to fainting goats and glue.

Someone had to make life interesting around here, to break up the routine of a North Dakotan existence. And I guess that someone was me. So, yeah, a day filled with goats and glued doors and staplers and pens would be totally worth it compared to just another day. I mean, sometimes even my pranks weren't enough. Which is I guess why they just kept getting bigger and bigger. Heck, by the time I graduated eighth grade, I'd probably have to resort to filling the entire school with foamy soap suds, escaped mental patients, and ravenous grizzly bears wearing slippery shoes just to make things seem slightly more exciting than a teeth cleaning at the dentist's office.

Gomez and I arrived at his office and I held my breath as he reached for the doorknob, expecting it to already be glued shut. It opened without any resistance. So they hadn't gotten to his door yet. I was both utterly relieved and bitterly disappointed. It had taken a lot of planning and work and favors to get a whole herd of fainting goats to the school. And now, despite how funny it had all been, I wouldn't even get to see the real payoff. But at least my friends had gotten away without getting caught. They must have seen Gomez apprehend me from his office window and had taken off. Hopefully they were still inside the school gluing all the other stuff we planned while the rest of the school staff was outside trying to somehow regain control of wild herds of goats and kids and parents.

Principal Gomez's office is always smaller than I expect. I remember that was the first thing I noticed when I made my first visit there last year as a sixth grader. Since then, I'd sat in the small chair across from his desk tons of times, so I'd gotten used to the claustrophobic death trap that he called an office.

After glancing out his window at the herd of fainting goats on the school's front lawn, Mr. Gomez sighed, shook his head, and sat down.

"What is that, exactly?" he said, nodding at the brown package sitting on my lap.

I shrugged and placed it on the chair next to me.

"Open it," he said, while wrinkles of paranoia formed on his sweaty forehead, just above his beady and suspicious eyes.

Mr. Gomez was one of the most paranoid people I'd ever met. I could only imagine how it was at his house—he probably grilled his wife with forty questions every time she sneezed. "What was that? A secret message? A signal? Are you plotting something? Who are you working with?" Then she'd roll her eyes like always, and say, "It's just dusty. Why don't you ever clean around here?" And he'd say back, "Because the dirt, it keeps the *ants* away. Don't you know they're trying to get in here and steal our food? You can't expect me to just let the ants run the show, can you? Are you in cahoots with the ants? Is that it?"

Okay, he probably wasn't that bad, but it still wouldn't surprise me. He did like to use the word *cahoots* a lot, though. Which always made me laugh.

"Well? Open it," he said, his eyes shuffling continuously back and forth between me and the package as if one of us might get away if he took his eyes off us for longer than three seconds.

And whatever you do, don't open it!

The guy in the suit's words echoed in my brain. I'd seen plenty of James Bond movies. Visions flooded my mind of me opening the package and releasing a deadly yellow gas that would infect the whole school in under ten seconds and then quickly spread to neighboring towns. I wasn't as paranoid as Gomez, but I also wasn't going to be the guy responsible for destroying the country, that much was for sure. Even if it would be kind of exciting for something that big to happen around here.

"I can't," I said.

"Why not?"

I had a dilemma. I couldn't tell the truth, obviously. Somehow the words *it might be deadly* didn't seem like they'd go over too well with Mr. Gomez. And also saying something like *some strange guy gave it to me outside and I don't know what's in it* didn't seem like it'd work much better. In fact, almost everything I could think of would only make him more likely to make me open it.

Mr. Gomez scowled and squinted at me so hard that

his eyes seemed to shrink back inside his head as if they were running from something. I needed to think quickly. This was headed in the wrong direction.

"It's my science project," I blurted out. "We had to study the habituation of compound odiferous emissions; and so my project studies how seven-week-old rotten eggs will interact with dog poop in a confined and sealed space. A virtual vacuum, you see. So, if I were to open it now, not only would it ruin the results, but the noxious fumes may just kill us both."

Mr. Gomez made a face. "That's disgusting. Who is your science teacher? I don't want—"

But he didn't get to finish his sentence because the phone rang. He grabbed the receiver and tried to answer—but it didn't budge. He pulled harder and the whole phone lifted up off the desk, still ringing. I tried desperately to suppress a laugh. Apparently Dillon and Danielle had at least gotten started gluing stuff in here.

Mr. Gomez glared at me, and I could tell he knew that I was somehow responsible for this. He put the phone down and held it there with one hand and then gripped and yanked hard at the receiver with the other. There was a crack as the glue bond broke and the receiver shot up and hit him in the face.

He turned red and rubbed his nose before putting the phone up to his ear.

"Yeah?" he practically yelled, clearly annoyed. "I don't know . . . round them up. Put them . . . put them in the faculty lounge for all I care. Just get them off the school lawn!"

I had almost forgotten about the goats.

"Call animal services!" Mr. Gomez screamed into the phone. "Make them into goat curry. . . . I don't care! Just get them off school property!"

There would be no need to call animal services. The goats were from Dillon and Danielle's uncle's farm, and their older cousin, Brad, would show up soon with a trailer to pick up the goats and spin some story about how he was driving them through town and happened to be parked nearby when the trailer latch suddenly broke and the animals ran free. I was lucky Brad had such a good sense of humor. Not many twenty-two-year-olds would loan out a whole herd of fainting goats for a prank. But he had a history of his own with Mr. Gomez from back in the day, and I guess some grudges ran longer than your standard three years at Eric Hill Middle School.

Through the window behind Mr. Gomez, I saw people running back and forth across the school lawn, still chasing a few last goats. It was funny because fainting goats really aren't all that hard to herd places, but I suppose these teachers were used to herding kids, not goats.

Mr. Gomez slammed down the phone and glared at me.

"Now, you want to tell me how you managed to get those goats here? And why my phone was glued together?"

"What goats?" I said.

"Ah!" He yelled in frustration. "You know which goats, Mr. Fender."

Of course he knew it was me. It was always me. But like usual, he didn't have any proof. We'd both been through this drill before: He'd call me in here and yell at me for a while; I'd stay firm and plead ignorance; and then he'd give me two weeks of detention. Without proof he couldn't suspend or expel me. Technically he couldn't give me detention either. But I just took it, every time. I mean, I was actually guilty, so why would I argue too much with detention? It was better than expulsion. It was kind of like an understanding between Gomez and me. A plea bargain of sorts. We both knew I was guilty, and we both knew he could never prove it, so instead of getting parents and other administration involved, we always just settled on twenty minutes of me being shouted at and two weeks of detention. It had become like everything else in this town: just another boring and meaningless routine that played itself out over and over again.

At least he had forgotten about the package.

"I've never seen those goats before," I said.

"We both know that's a lie! I'm tired of this, Carson. When are you going to learn your lesson? Huh?"

It went on like this for a while. Him lecturing me, and me denying everything. Then he got angrier and yelled, and then a little calmer. And then he went through his usual paranoia stage where he assumed that this prank was just a diversion for a larger one that was happening elsewhere in the school right at that moment. (Which, to be fair to Mr. Gomez, was precisely what was happening.)

And then we were near the end.

"That'll be another two weeks detention, Carson," Mr. Gomez said, breathing heavily and writing something down. (He'd had to pry the pen and notebook off his desk.)

"For what?" I said, playing my part like always. "I didn't do anything."

"You want to make that three?"

I knew it was a bluff—it always was. He didn't want to push his luck. I could fight back, after all, and tell my parents, and then the superintendent would get involved and it would be a huge mess. Neither of us wanted that. So I played into his bluff like always.

"No, sir."

"Good. You may go now."

And just like that, it was over.

10010110101000001010100101010100100000
1010100100100101010010100010101001010
1010100001001010010101010010101010101010101
000101010101010100110010101010101010101010
10101010101000001010010101010010101010100
10101000010010100101010010101010101010101
0001   00110010101010101010101010
010   0010101010010101010101001
10   1010100101010101010101

CHAPTER 3

AFTER DETENTION, I MET UP WITH DILLON, DANIELLE, ZACK, AND
Ethan by the school's football field. I still had the package, of course, but at the moment I was more concerned
about how much they'd glued down and if any of them
had gotten caught. They usually helped me with my
pranks, especially Dillon and Danielle, who were twin
brother and sister. And they got detention from time to
time. But I was usually the guy taking the fall. And I liked
it that way. They were *my* master plans after all.

"What's that?" Dillon asked, pointing at the package.

"Is that like some sort of secret delivery that you have to make for a mob boss? Or did *they* finally get to you?"

Ethan, Danielle, and Zack all groaned, but I merely marveled at how close he might actually be to the truth. That guy in the suit could have been some mobster or something. I mean, I still had no idea who he was, or what was in the package.

But that was the thing about my best friend, Dillon. There was always a "they." He was a conspiracy theorist, which basically meant that he was always convinced there was something fishy going on with absolutely everything at absolutely all times. And it changed from week to week as to who the "they" he was ranting about actually were. Sometimes it was aliens taking over the planet, sometimes it was microscopic robots, created by the government, that get inside our brains to control us, and other times it was Icelandic spies determined to take down the US so they could use our land to bury millions of cubes of Mako shark meat and then dig it up months later to eat it.

It was one of the things I loved most about Dillon, though. Sure it could get annoying sometimes, since he never let up and was always trying to get me to go investigate his theories with him, but most of the time it was too funny and interesting and *different* to be anything but entertaining. I mean, at least he envisioned this town being something more than what it was. And at least he said stuff that nobody else did. He didn't just talk about what funny videos he watched on YouTube last night or who was going out with who, like pretty much everybody else. When he talked, it was usually something unexpected, even if it probably was made up.

Once, for about a week, Dillon was convinced that his younger sister was really a demon and was trying to kill him in his sleep by cramming Lucky Charms marshmallows into his ears. Or, even just last week, he tried to convince me that he saw some spy dressed as a lion tamer snooping around the water treatment plant across from the school. Another time he told me he found out that Walmart was really a secret front for a huge, international monkey-smuggling ring. That one was pretty far-fetched, even for him.

"Monkeys?" I had said.

"Yeah, monkeys."

"Don't you mean like drugs or guns or something?"

"No," he said. "Monkeys. You know, for like secret drug testing and genetic experiments and illegal pets and stuff. They got to get the monkeys from somewhere, right? Now let's go, we gotta go check it out!"

"Dillon, I'm not going to Walmart on a Saturday. That's where everybody goes on Saturdays, including the weirdos. The things I've seen in that place on Saturdays haunt my dreams!"

"But the monkeys!"

I had just laughed at this. Dillon's faced had remained grim. It was funny, sure, but he always took it seriously. He always used to say to me, "Yeah, you can laugh now, but one day you'll see. You think the whole world really operates on the level?"

It was the same look he was giving me now, his eyes constantly flicking back to the package under my arm.

"This? This is nothing, just something I was supposed to bring to the school office today from my parents but forgot to," I said, holding up the package. "I'm assuming since you're all here that you got away safely?"

"Yeah," Danielle, Dillon's twin sister, said. "We glued stuff in at least thirty classrooms and even more doors and lockers and nobody even saw us."

"Yeah, that goat thing was perfect!" Zack said. "The teachers all panicked and rushed outside. The school was deserted."

"I still wish I'd gotten to see it, though. The goats, I

mean," Dillon said, seeming to have accepted my explanation of the package. For now.

"Don't worry, I'm pretty sure at least a dozen kids caught it on their phones and it will be posted on YouTube by tonight, if it isn't already," I said. "Well, thanks again, guys. It'll be hilarious tomorrow when everyone realizes what the real prank was. I gotta run or I'll miss my bus."

We said our good-byes and I jogged back toward the front of the school where the buses picked up each day.

I carried the package carefully on the bus and the walk home from where the bus dropped off. I debated putting it in my backpack, but it didn't fit and I didn't want to have to cram it inside. So instead I carried it under one arm like a football.

"Dude, nice job, with the goats and everything," my brother Austin said almost as soon as I walked in the door.

He was entrenched on the couch as usual, his pants crumpled on the floor. I never understood why my older brother was so obsessed with walking around in his boxers all the time. But it was the first thing he did every day when he got home—take off his jeans, grab a soda, find the couch. Maybe it was just what every guy does after high school?

"You heard about that already?"

He laughed. "Yeah, everybody has heard about it. The whole town, practically."

I nodded and couldn't hide my grin, especially since it wouldn't be until tomorrow that everyone understood what the true prank was.

Austin grinned back. "Nice work, brother. I bet the top of Gomez's head blew off right there on the spot."

"Yeah, he was pretty mad," I said. "It was awesome."

Austin nodded. "I bet. I mean, I'll never forget the look on his face that one time I turned his office into a swimming pool. When— Hey, what's that?"

He pointed at the package tucked under my arm.

"Oh, nothing," I said, trying to play it cool.

Austin squinted and tilted his head. "No, really, what's in there? Let me see it."

"Nah, I'll just be . . ." I started, but then suddenly he was on his feet and blocking the route to the stairs.

"What's in the package?" he asked again.

My brother is a curious guy. Nosy is probably a better word for it. He didn't like to miss out on anything that even had a remote chance of being fun, funny, or totally and completely reckless and dangerous. All three was the jackpot of course. And a mysterious package had possibilities.

Instead of answering, I held the package out to my left. When his eyes followed it, I darted quickly to my right. He reacted fast, but I had caught him off guard and so he overcompensated. That's when I did a quick spin back to my left and I was past him just like that.

I backpedaled through the kitchen toward the stairs holding the package out in front of me. "Sorry, it's top secret," I said with a triumphant smile.

He didn't pursue me but instead just grinned and then plopped himself back down onto the couch.

"Hey," he called just as I'd started down the stairs to the basement where my room was, "I'm going to the circus tonight with some friends; you and Dillon and Danielle want to come?"

The circus always came to town for a few weeks at the beginning of every school year. Except it was more like a circus–fair hybrid with rides and games and stuff in addition to the giant tent and acrobats and elephants. It was sort of a tradition that we went at least once every year, sometimes more. Pretty much every kid in town did.

It used to be the thing that I looked forward to the most. For those two weeks every year there was actually something cool to do in town. There were rides and games and animals and weirdo carnies around. We all liked to play a game we called "Guess Which Carnie Is Secretly a Serial Killer."

But then I noticed, starting around fifth grade, that even the circus had begun to feel like a part of the North Dakota routine to me. It was just another section of the track that we were all on. I still went, and it was still fun. But it definitely wasn't the same as it used to be. In fact, the simple truth that it was still the most exciting thing to happen around here every year almost made it feel worse. Like, if this was as exciting as things got around here, then we were all doomed.

"Mom made you ask me?" I said, knowing that no eighteen-year-old kid would really ever want his little brother and his friends tagging along.

He just rolled his eyes in response.

I was tempted to say yes, but the thought of abandoning the mysterious package in my closet didn't seem like a very good idea. I mean, what if that guy really was a mobster? And his cronies came looking for the package? I didn't want to be responsible for getting my parents whacked or something. My dad was already a terrible swimmer, and wearing a pair of concrete shoes certainly wouldn't help much.

"Nah, I have stuff to do," I said. "Aren't you a little old for the circus anyway?"

"Yeah, well, there are, uh, ways to make pretty much anything fun," he said.

I nodded, despite not really knowing what he meant exactly and then went downstairs to my room and hid the package in my closet.

CHAPTER 4

I WAS AFTER DINNER NOW AND DARK OUTSIDE. I WAS BACK IN my room. And I had a problem.

I swear, before that moment, I really had no desire to open the package. Mostly because of what the sweaty guy in formal wear had said earlier that day when he'd handed it to me: *And whatever you do, don't open it!*

Suddenly, though, alone in my room, with the day's events behind me, staring at the simple brown paper wrapping, I was dying to know what was inside. Was it secret documents? A box of old worthless baseball cards? Maybe the whole thing had been an elaborate counter-prank orchestrated by Dillon?

I was so distracted during dinner that I almost blew my cover about the goats when my mom asked if I'd heard about it. Unsurprisingly, it had made the local news. Around here a herd of goats at a local middle school was prime Top Story material.

After she asked me about it, I shook my head innocently. Then I said something like, "Goats in a school? That's crazy!"

Which made my brother laugh so hard that he spit a chunk of green bean right into my glass of milk. Which of course had then made me fling a bean back at Austin and then my dad started yelling at everyone to settle down.

But now here I was, back in my room, staring at the package and wishing I had X-ray vision or something. It dawned on me just then that this little brown package was the single most exciting and mysterious thing to ever come into my life. It sat on my bed and the moonlight coming in through my one small window made the brown wrapper almost glow. As if it was actually alive, taunting me.

Open me.

Come on, open me.

"I'd better not. That guy said . . ."

Ah, he doesn't know what he's talking about. Don't you want to know what's inside? How bad could it be?

"Um, I don't know—you could be filled with a deadly gas, which I could release into the atmosphere and cause the zombie apocalypse."

Pfft. What are the odds that really ends up being true? This is North Dakota; that kind of stuff doesn't happen here. You know that.

The package had a good point.

"The thing is . . ."

"Carson," my mom said from outside my room, "who are you talking to in there?"

Had I been talking out loud to the package?

"Nobody," I said, hoping I didn't sound as crazy as I probably was.

"Well, okay," she said, sounding unconvinced. Nonetheless, I heard her walk down the hall to the laundry room.

Who are you calling a nobody?

"It doesn't matter what you say, I'm not opening you," I whispered.

There could be money inside, did you ever think of that?

The truth was I hadn't thought of that. There *could* be money inside after all. In the movies, the mysterious packages that were exchanged in business deals and delivered by couriers always contained either money or . . . well, drugs.

Look at it this way. You could either not open me and deliver me to Mr. Jensen like the guy said to and then that will be that—you can go back to your same old North Dakota life and nothing at all will be different. You'll still go to school and sit through boring lectures and take pointless tests so you can go to college and take even more tests all so you can get a job working in some tiny office here in town with a boss who plays solitaire all day long and goes bowling every other Tuesday night to add excitement to his life.

"Or?"

Or you could open me right here and now and see what's inside and potentially find something that could change your life forever. Or at least make for an exciting couple of days.

The package made another good point. What I'd seen that day after school had been so unexpected, so utterly non–North Dakotan, that my brain had barely even been able to register that it had happened at all. And now here I was, with a chance to somehow become a part of whatever crazy thing was going on, with a chance to actually break the routine for once.

Well?

"I'm thinking. Give me a second."

The package just stared at me. And so we were back to this. It looked so unassuming, sitting there wrapped up all neatly in its brown paper.

I mean, if it was something dangerous, then why was it being delivered to a school? In September, in North Dakota? And what about those pasty-faced guys? No, this probably had to be a prank of some sort, anyway. It was just the sort of ridiculous thing that made for good pranks. In the end, it was just too good to be true. There was no way it was real—it would be just too cool of a thing to actually be happening here.

I never thought you'd end up being such a chicken.

"That's not fair, Package."

There was a long pause.

Bok.

Bok-bok-bok.

"That's not going to work, you know. I'm not eight years old anymore."

Bok. Bok-bok-bok. Bok-BOK-bok-bok.

"Fine!"

I scooted my chair over toward the bed and picked up the package. I carefully lifted up the end flaps, picking at the tape first so I didn't tear the paper. Though I'm not sure why I thought that suddenly mattered since I was now doing exactly what the guy in the suit had told me not to.

Underneath the brown paper wrapping was a box. It was black and rectangular, slightly smaller than a shoe box, and about half as thick. There were no markings on the outside of any kind. The cold surface seemed to be made of metal and at first it didn't look as though it had a lid, or any seams at all for that matter. But then I saw the small quarter-size ring resting inside a shallow indentation.

A handle.

I looped my index finger through the ring and pulled. It didn't budge.

What are you trying to do, pick my nose? Put some muscle into it!

I had thought the package was done taunting me.

I grabbed the edge of the box with my free hand and tightened my grip on the little ring. I held my breath, then gave it a good, hard yank, as if I were trying to start an old lawnmower. This time there was a click. The lid swung open.

But I'd actually pulled too hard and so I lost my grip and my balance and sprawled back onto the floor, tipping over my chair.

And then, from the floor, I heard a woman's voice rise out from the black box still sitting on my bed. A real voice this time. One that actually talked to me aloud.

"Hello," the box said.

CHAPTER 5

I SLOWLY GOT TO MY FEET. I WASN'T EVEN SURE THAT I REALLY wanted to see what was inside. A real live lawn gnome? A spirit that I'd just freed after years of captivity? A talking shoe with a beard?

But it wasn't any of those things; it was nothing alive at all. Inside the box, just below the surface, was an LCD screen. Its display was entirely blue, except for this message in white letters:

Touch Here to Continue . . .

I just stood there and looked at the blue screen for a while. I wasn't even trying to figure out what to do. My brain was too shocked to process or entertain those kinds of thoughts. So mostly I was just gaping at it.

Then it spoke again and I nearly jumped right through my ceiling and into the kitchen one floor above me.

"Please touch the screen to continue."

The woman's voice was friendly and polite, a little robotic. It sounded just like any other automated voice I'd heard before. Like the ones that play over the intercom at the airport, repeating the same messages over and over again.

If this was a prank, it was elaborate. Too elaborate. For the first time, I realized, I was really, truly considering that this might be real. That the sweaty guy in the suit really was serious about this box being important and that I was suddenly in possession of something I had no business being in possession of. But I also had to admit that I liked the possibility that this was real. For the first time pretty much ever, I truly didn't know what was going to happen next. Just sitting there staring at a metal box had suddenly become the most exciting thing I'd ever done, as strange as that sounds. Even more exciting than when Dillon and I snuck onto the Zipper for the very first time at the circus when we were in fourth grade.

There really was only one option at this point, the way I saw it. After all, I had already opened the box, which the courier had specifically told me not to do.

I reached out and touched the screen with my index finger.

"Thank you," said the box and then the screen went black.

I wasn't sure what to do next. My mind began to run wild with all sorts of crazy things I might have just initiated by pressing the button on the screen. Like maybe I'd just launched ten nuclear missiles at Denmark. I had no idea why anyone would want to bomb Denmark, but my mind wasn't exactly working rationally just then. Or maybe I'd just activated a huge killer robot that shoots swarms of killer bees out of its eyes and had been living below Disneyland and now it would rise up and turn the earth into a huge ball of honeycomb.

But then the woman's voice started speaking again. The words she spoke scrolled across the screen. And had I not been able to read them for myself, I might not have believed what she told me next. I would have assumed I'd misheard. I definitely wouldn't have wanted to believe it, anyway.

Warning! An unauthorized non-Agency user has been detected. You have just successfully activated the Data File Security System™. This data system will automatically self-destruct in 48 hours if the fail-safe procedures are not initiated. Any further unauthorized attempt to access the data or tamper with the system's hardware will result in immediate self-destruction.

My eyes kept passing back over the word *destruction*. Then all of the words disappeared and were replaced by a large digital clock.

48:00:00

47:59:59

47:59:58

I rubbed my eyes and blinked a few times just to make sure I wasn't hallucinating.

47:59:54

Nope. It was real.

47:59:52

What had I just done?

CHAPTER 6

THERE IS NOT MUCH OF A CHANCE THAT I WOULD HAVE BEEN able to get any sleep after activating a top secret self-destructing data device. But even that small chance was wiped out by the fact that the device insisted on reminding me over and over what I'd done in its polite voice.

"You now have forty-six hours and forty-five minutes to initiate fail-safe measures before self-destruction," the voice said to me.

I found out after the first hour that the voice reminded whatever moron (i.e., me) who happened to have opened the box and now happened to be hanging around listening just how much time was left every fifteen minutes. And who knows what would happen when the counter reached zero? What did "self-destruct" really mean, anyway? Would it actually explode like a bomb? Or just, like, fry its own internal hardware? I'd already considered just dumping the box somewhere, but what if it did actually explode at the end of the forty-eight hours? Even if I left it in a Dumpster, or in the middle of a field, who's to say that some kid or farmer wouldn't happen to find it with only ten seconds left in the countdown or something?

Plus, all of that isn't even mentioning the fact that the computer most likely contained highly sensitive and important information that someone needed to see for the safety of the whole country. Why else would it have such serious countermeasures?

So I'd placed the device on my desk and stared at it while trying to figure out what to do. An hour after I opened it I was still sitting there staring at it—no closer to an answer than I had been sixty minutes before. I made a mental note that the next time some harried and panicked guy in a suit gave me directions, I would probably follow them, no matter how cool or exciting the alternative seemed.

And whatever you do, don't open it!

Idiot! I thought to myself.

"You now have forty-six hours and thirty minutes to initiate fail-safe measures before self-destruction."

"Shut up, Betsy!" I yelled at it. "I know how much time I have!"

I'd decided to name the computer Betsy. Because the shrewdly calm and passive-aggressive diabolical voice reminded me of this girl named Betsy in my second-period class who was always tattling on kids. Or bragging about how her dad got two free tickets to the Super Bowl, or how her dad was going to buy her a car when she was in ninth grade. Or about how their house had a four-car garage, which was super rare. Or making comments about some other girl's ugly shoes. Or blah, blah, blah.

Then I heard my dad thundering down the stairs. He stopped at my door and knocked in a way that was just short of pounding.

"Carson, what are you yelling about? Go to bed! I have a flight at five in the morning!"

"Sorry, Dad," I said. He traveled a lot for his job and was awake before the sun came up most mornings.

He didn't answer me and I heard his heavy footsteps marching back upstairs to my parents' bedroom. Their door shut and then the house was mostly quiet again.

I closed the box and put it inside my lower desk drawer. Maybe I just needed to sleep on it. Tomorrow morning I'd know what to do. I climbed into bed, trying to think of some way I could go back and undo the past twelve hours.

But even through the closed metal lid and the drawer, I could still hear Betsy:

"You now have forty-six hours and fifteen minutes to initiate fail-safe measures before self-destruction."

The volume was muffled, but Betsy's sharp words still cut right through me like hot shrapnel. I got out of bed and scrambled over to the desk, grabbing Betsy with the intention of putting her up on my windowsill. And that's when I saw it out my ground-level basement window.

A dark sedan with tinted windows rolled slowly past the front of my house. Too slowly. Our street was residential and didn't get much traffic this time of night. The car didn't stop moving, but it was going so slow it was almost as if it wasn't even moving at all.

There was something else extremely sinister about the car, but I couldn't put my finger on what it was. I mean, it was the same kind that had apprehended the guy in the suit, and sure it had windows tinted so dark they were like black souls spilled around the glass, and yeah the car was moving so slowly the driver was probably using the brake to accelerate it. All of that was definitely creepy. But even beyond that stuff, there was something else that felt wrong about it.

I tried shaking it off as I shoved the black box into the back of my closet. It would likely be less audible there than on my high windowsill anyway. I peeked outside again; the car was gone. Somehow, that made things even worse. The shadows on my wall had never appeared to be so cold and uncaring. They looked like they wanted to turn me in, like they were pointing the dark sedan right to me.

So this is what it must be like to be Mr. Gomez.

"You now have forty-six hours to initiate fail-safe measures before self-destruction."

The closet didn't do much to muffle Betsy's words. I was never going to get to sleep again, I decided—tonight and tomorrow because of Betsy's announcements, and after that because I'd likely be locked up in some supersecret government prison in Siberia or something.

I got up and piled my spare blanket on top of Betsy. Then my comforter. Then my spare pillow. Try talking through that, Betsy.

Before getting back into bed, I looked out the window again. And my heart slowly sank down into my right leg where it bounced past my knee and eventually plopped into my ankle area. Or at least that's what it felt like was happening.

The sedan was back, making another pass down my street. And this time, I noticed what it was that made it so menacing: Its headlights were off. It was pitch-black outside and the car's headlights were off. Who does that? Also, it had no license plates or make or model markings of any kind.

I quickly ducked down as the sedan rolled past our front yard. A bead of sweat trickled into my eye and clogged my vision momentarily. What was I going to do? Getting rid of Betsy would be even harder with whomever it was in that car creeping around my neighborhood. I mean, they had to be related, right?

But even if I could find a way to sneak Betsy out of here and into the school and past Mr. Gomez, there was a whole other problem.

The guy who handed it to me had told me to deliver it to Mr. Jensen. I didn't know if this thing was good or bad, if the information it held could be used to save the country or ruin it. But something about the way the guy had looked at me said that he was one of the good guys. That whatever was in the package was something important, something that couldn't fall into the wrong hands. I knew the only chance I had of finding out what that was was to get it to Mr. Jensen.

But that was the problem. Simply handing it to Mr. Jensen wouldn't be that easy.

Because there were two Mr. Jensens at my school.

One taught music, and the other taught sixth-grade social studies. They even spelled their names the same way. How was I supposed to know which one was the right one? And what would happen if I delivered the package to the wrong one?

I swallowed, hoping to ease this sudden urge I had to barf all over my pajamas. As much as I had to admit that all this was actually pretty exciting, it was also terrifying because I simply didn't feel like I was capable of handling it. I mean, this kind of stuff simply doesn't happen in North Dakota. The most exciting thing to happen around here is when some kid places fourth at the regional Midwest 4H Competition for matching the right calves to the right mother cows. Okay, that was an exaggeration, but only slightly. The point was the same, nothing that had ever happened to me before could have remotely prepared me for suddenly being in charge of some crazy top secret self-destructing computer files containing who knows what kinds of national secrets. I liked to shake things up, to pull pranks. But those pranks didn't actually come with any real consequences besides a little detention now and then.

"You now have forty-five hours and forty-five minutes to initiate fail-safe measures before self-destruction."

I sighed and sat down at the desk below my bedroom window. There was no point in even trying to sleep now. Betsy's voice was definitely softer under all those blankets, but it was still unmistakably the voice of real consequence. Which made it impossible to ignore.

01001011101010100000101010010101010100100000
010101001001001010101001010010101001010
10101000010010100101010100101010101010101
00001010101010101001100101010101010101010
01010101010100001010010101001010101000
10101000010010100101010100101010101010101
00001   001100101010101010101010
010   001010101001010101001
101   1010100101010101010101

CHAPTER 7

OKAY, LET ME JUST START OUT BY SAYING THAT I KNOW BRING-
ing a secret, mysterious device that may or may not be
dangerous to school is about the worst, dumbest, most
horrible thing a kid could do. But what else was I supposed to do with it the next day? Leave it at my house
for one of my parents to find? Call the cops and risk the
information not getting where it needed to go? I mean,
for all I knew the cops might be in on whatever kind of
shenanigans the guys in the dark sedan had going on
around here. In the movies, the local police are always

on the take. Or was I supposed to pay some random guy to watch it in the hope that he wasn't as stupid as I was— that he wouldn't try to figure out what was in the box? Or should I have just put it on my neighbor's stoop then rung the doorbell and run away? No, I couldn't possibly have done that to poor Mr. Sherman. The old guy could hardly even see anymore, and he was definitely deaf. So he'd have no idea that Betsy was potentially dangerous.

So, anyway, the point is that, yes, I had to bring Betsy to school. Even if it was just my bad luck for being where I was at the exact moment that guy in the suit showed up, it was my responsibility now. I couldn't put this one on my parents or anyone else.

Besides, to be honest, part of me didn't want to pass this off to someone else, even as scary as it was. Because then everything would go back to normal, and that almost seemed worse somehow.

When I woke that morning, if you could even call my tossing and turning "sleep," Betsy greeted me by saying, "You now have thirty-nine hours and fifteen minutes to initiate fail-safe measures before self-destruction." Reminding me both that last night was not some sort of crazy dream and also that the device itself had a habit of loudly announcing its existence every fifteen minutes.

The first challenge was getting it from my closet, onto the bus, and safely into my locker without anyone noticing. It wasn't like I could just cram it into my backpack and act like nothing was wrong when she started talking about imminent self-destruction. It wouldn't be easy to get a mysterious talking device into school, but I had a plan . . . of sorts.

I dug out an old digital wristwatch I'd gotten for my birthday a few years ago. Amazingly, the battery was still working. I switched it to timer mode and synched up the timer with Betsy's automated message. My first thought had been to just use the timer on my phone, but the problem with that was that I couldn't be looking at my phone all day in class. Our school had a policy that no phone could be seen at all by a teacher during class, or else it would be confiscated for the rest of the day.

After wrapping Betsy in one of my old T-shirts and stuffing it into my bag, I ran down to the corner to wait for the bus. As it approached, Betsy's slightly muffled voice in my backpack said, "You now have thirty-eight hours to initiate fail-safe measures before self-destruction."

"Wow, thanks, Betsy," I said under my breath as the bus squealed to a stop in front of me.

Grins, high fives, and fist bumps greeted me as I walked down the aisle. It took me a second to remember what that was about. Everyone in school must have known I was behind the fainting goat stunt yesterday. I'd honestly completely forgotten about that, you know, with the talking secret package and everything.

I sat down in an empty seat a few rows from the back.

"Hey, nice job yesterday," a seventh grader in the next seat over whispered. "That was hilarious. I mean, goats?"

"Thanks, just wait until you see what happens today when we get to school," I said distractedly.

Twelve minutes and six seconds until the next update from Betsy, according to my watch. The bus ride usually took at least fifteen minutes. I sat there and fidgeted as I watched us hit every single red light possible. There was no way I'd get my backpack off this bus before the next update.

At the next stop some kid sat down right next to me. If I'd been paying attention, I'd have stopped him before he did. But I'd been lost thinking about just what kind of secrets this thing might actually hold. Was it information about secret government facilities where aliens are experimented on? Did it contain the truth about who really shot JFK? Or the coordinates to the missing loot of

Billy the Kid? Would all that stuff really be lost forever if I wasn't able to deliver it before the timer reached zero?

Anyway, the kid who sat next to me was named Olek. He'd recently moved here from some country I'd never heard of. All I knew was that it had an *ia* on the end. I think it was Lastonia or something like that. I'd heard from other kids that he was weird. Like, really weird. But he seemed okay to me. Besides, I usually liked the weird kids. My best friend was a genuine conspiracy theorist after all. To me, *weird* simply meant *interesting*, as in something different from the same old North Dakota stuff, where it seemed like everybody aspired only to be just like everybody else. Sometimes it seemed like every kid here could have been swapped at birth with some other random kid and nobody's parents would notice and it wouldn't have made any difference to how we all turned out.

Anyway, I suppose it could have been worse. It could have been the real Betsy who'd sat down next to me on the bus. She'd totally have grilled me about what I was hiding in my bag and then eventually tattle on me like always.

"Greetings," said Olek, in a thick accent.

"Hi," I said, and instinctively pulled the backpack closer to me.

He must have noticed, because he glanced at the bag and then asked, "What's in bag?"

"What do you mean?"

"You guard like you have gold pieces inside, yes?"

I tried to shrug it off casually. "No, Olek, I'm just anxious to get to school, that's all. There's nothing inside here but books. And pens. And some pencils. Yep, just full of normal school stuff, that's all. Nothing else. Nothing unusual whatsoever."

I gave my bag a pat to show that it was just a normal old backpack.

"Oh-leck," he said.

"Huh?"

"My name, is say Oh-leck. Not Ah-lick. Oh-leck."

"Oh, I'm sorry. Olek."

"It's not problem," he said, and grinned.

Then he took out a phone and started playing some game or texting someone. I breathed out slowly and checked my watch. Just six minutes left. Then five. Then two. We were still nowhere near the school. The minutes on my watch slowly bled away until there were only ten seconds left.

I looked around. The bus was pretty full and the kids talkative enough, but it was still too quiet. The kids in the seats around me definitely would hear Betsy and maybe, if it happened at just the right time, the bus driver would, too. Then it'd be game over for sure.

Seven seconds.

Six.

I shoved my bag as far under my seat as it would go. I put my legs in front of it.

Three seconds.

I took a deep breath.

One.

"OOOOOHHHH, beneath a mist of corndog," I sang (or shouted is likely more accurate) as loudly as I could, "I have found a sack o' mang, it's overture collaboration is of horticulture thang!"

At first the kids were quiet, but then they all started laughing before joining me for the second verse of the song. Last year at the end of our homecoming assembly, I had switched these new lyrics with our school song's real lyrics on the PowerPoint presentation that they projected onto a big screen. It took a few passes before kids noticed, but once they did, they started singing my new lyrics instead of the real ones. Principal Gomez eventually realized what was happening and shut off the projector, but it was too late. The whole school had been roaring by that point.

Anyway, later that week I had the modified lyrics distributed around the school so kids could learn them. For the next several assemblies every kid in the school sang the new lyrics instead of the real ones. Now, they don't even play our school song at assemblies anymore. But we all still sing "Beneath a Mist o' Corndog" at every sporting event. Although Gomez would never admit it, I think it actually gave kids more school spirit than the old lyrics did. Besides, the old lyrics were the same as when my parents went to school here.

As the bus finished the fourth verse of the song and everyone laughed, I realized that I had been loud enough so that even I hadn't heard Betsy give her most recent time update. It had worked. Of course, the bus would be the easy part. The bus driver didn't much care what we did as long as we stayed seated. Hiding Betsy's constant updates during school would be a whole different challenge.

"Why you sing song on bus?" Olek asked.

"A school custom," I said.

He made a face like we were all crazy. "Ah," he said. "Okay. In my country we sometimes sing, too."

I nodded. "Yeah? Cool."

"Yes, but our songs much better. In our country we mostly sing Jimmy Buffett song."

"Who's Jimmy Buffett?" I asked.

Olek's jaw hung open. He looked as if I'd just told him I didn't know who Abraham Lincoln was or something.

"You not know Jimmy Buffett?"

"No, should I?"

"Yes, of course, he is like American cowboy plus hippie on desert island. In my country he is hero. Jimmy Buffett song replace our national anthem and he has statue in Logan Square in our capital city."

"Wow, you guys really love this Jimmy Buffett dude. He must be pretty good."

Olek nodded wildly. "Yes! Yes, he is like . . . like musical diamond sauce!"

I looked at him and even in spite of the device under my seat I laughed and then clapped Olek on the shoulder to make sure he knew I wasn't laughing at him. After a few seconds, he grinned and then started laughing himself.

CHAPTER 8

DILLON WAS WAITING FOR ME AT MY LOCKER WHEN I GOT TO school.

"That was so hilarious yesterday," he said with a grin. "You were right about YouTube. There was one video posted that shows Mrs. Kingsley tripping over one of the goats and doing a full somersault. Her long jean skirt flipped all the way over her head and you could see her old lady granny underwear! It was so gross! But funny."

I laughed, but I was barely listening. I glanced at my

watch. I only had ninety-seven seconds before the next update.

"Hey! Last night, I think I saw a bearded lady smuggling a cache of weapons into the Burger King near my house. How weird is that? You want to come check it out with me after school?"

"No, I don't think so," I said.

"Whatever," he said. He usually gave up pretty easily since I basically never went with him to investigate his crazy theories.

"What's wrong? You're acting weird."

"Nothing, just distracted by this test I have in a little bit," I said.

"What? Since when have you ever been worried about a test?" Dillon asked, clearly not buying my terrible lie. "Did it finally happen? I knew it! I knew it was inevitable. *They* finally got to you, didn't they?"

"Not now, Dillon," I groaned. "Of course *they* didn't get to me. Look, I gotta go."

I shoved my bag into my locker and started walking away, desperate to get him away from Betsy's countdown. He followed me, but then stopped when he heard Betsy's voice drifting out of my locker, much louder than I would have expected. The acoustics inside the small metal locker were apparently concert-worthy.

"You now have thirty-seven hours and thirty minutes to initiate fail-safe measures before self-destruction."

Dillon looked at me, his mouth gaping open. "What was that?"

Well, that answered that, at least. There was no way I could keep Betsy in my locker today. Someone passing by would hear her for sure at some point. I was starting to think that bringing Betsy to school might have been the stupidest thing I'd ever done. Even stupider than opening Betsy in the first place. At least then I hadn't known what I was going to find. But with this, I'd known exactly what I was getting myself into.

"Hey, seriously, what was that?" Dillon repeated, as he walked back toward my locker.

I put my arm around his shoulder and tried to turn him back around. "It's just a little something for my next prank."

"Yeah, but did it just say something about destruction?"

"No, no, it said *instruction*. You'll see what that means when the time comes."

Dillon nodded as we walked away from my locker, but he still seemed unsure and kept sneaking glances back.

"When are you going to execute it and what can I do to help?"

"I'll let you know," I said as we parted ways down opposite ends of the hallway toward our first classes. "See you at lunch."

When I got to homeroom, everyone was standing outside the closed door. Our teacher, Ms. Larimore, was pulling on it furiously and it wouldn't open. That's because it had been one of the ones they'd gotten glued shut yesterday. The kids cheered when Ms. Larimore finally gave up.

"Wait here, all of you," she said and then marched off down the hallway.

I noticed that several other classes were standing around in the hallway, their doors glued shut as well. Kids were talking and laughing and I saw several of them wave at me. I just gave them a subtle nod in return.

Ms. Larimore returned a few minutes later with the janitor, who had a bucket of smelly goo with him. It must have been some sort of glue solvent because a short time after he painted the goop all over our door, our teacher was finally able to open it.

As we filed inside the classroom, I glanced at my watch. I had just over nine minutes to get back to my locker and get Betsy out of there before the next update. Homeroom still didn't let out for eleven minutes, which was obviously a problem.

I walked up to Ms. Larimore's desk. She glanced back and forth between the class and her computer, taking attendance. I could tell she was already in a bad mood from the door thing.

"Can I go to the bathroom?" I asked.

"I don't know, *can* you?" she said without looking at me.

I rolled my eyes. *"May I* go to the bathroom? Please."

"No."

Ms. Larimore was ancient. Therefore she had an old-school style of teaching. Which meant no talking, no bathroom breaks, no doodling, no doing anything that might remotely be fun and/or humane. She'd probably still whack kids in the face with a heavy oak stick like my grandpa used to talk about if the administration would let her get away with it. Pretty much the only things she hated worse than kids having fun were rodents. This one time a kid brought his pet gerbil to school, and when Ms. Larimore saw it in her classroom she screamed so loud, her coffee cup supposedly shattered. Then she kicked the kid and his pet out of her class, but not before giving him two weeks' detention.

"But . . . ," I started.

"You can wait ten minutes until class is over, can't you?" she said, finally looking at me.

"No, I really can't . . . I have to go . . ."

"You will, or else you'll be marching straight down to the principal's office."

I took a breath and glanced at my watch again. I had no choice. There was only one way she was going to let me out of here in time. I had to do the unimaginable. I clenched my teeth and waited.

Then I started to well tears in my eyes to draw her attention back toward me, like all good pranksters know how to do on command. At first she made a face like she was going to tell me to "grow up and stop blubbering" as I'd heard her say to other kids who had cried in class before. But then her eyes drifted down to my newly peed-in pants and she gasped.

"Oh, for Pete's sake! It's, that's, I mean, good heavens!" she sputtered, having a hard time grasping the reality of what had just happened. This was definitely outside the realm of a typical school day in North Dakota. "Get out of here and go clean yourself up, Carson! That's utterly revolting."

I turned and left the classroom. Thanks to Ms. Larimore's reaction, most of the kids in class had figured out what happened. Some laughed, some covered their mouths, and others just looked too shocked to react at all. But the ones laughing weren't laughing at me, at least not in that way. Most of them were likely laughing at my antics, assuming this was all part of some elaborate prank. It's one of the perks of being the school's best prankster; it gives you a long leash for actually making a fool out of yourself. If it were anyone else but me oozing out of class with wet pants right now, they'd be committing social suicide.

Nonetheless, having urine-soaked pants still felt disgusting.

I looked at my watch as I left the classroom. I had just enough time to run to the boys' locker room, throw on an extra pair of jeans and boxers I kept in my gym locker (sometimes pranks get messy), and get back to my normal locker before Betsy's next warning.

After changing clothes, I arrived at my locker with forty-six seconds to spare.

But my arrival just happened to be at the exact same moment as Mr. Gomez's.

1001101101010100000101010010101001001000
9101010010010010101010010100101010010100100101010
1010100001001010010101010010101010101010101
90001010101010101001100101010101010101010
910101010101000010100101010010101010100
101010000100101001010100101010101010101
90001   0011001010101010101010
9010   001010101001010101001
101   CHAPTER 9   1010100101010101010101

"I HEARD YOU HAD AN ACCIDENT IN HOMEROOM," HE SAID THE way someone might say it if they suspected it wasn't an accident at all.

I looked at my watch. Forty-two seconds.

"Yeah, too much OJ this morning," I said. "It was pretty embarrassing."

"Was it, though?" he asked, his shifty eyes bouncing back and forth inside their sockets like Ping-Pong balls.

I tried to casually check my watch, because, I mean, after all, what kid checks their watch every five seconds?

Not that many kids even wear watches at all for that matter.

Thirty-four seconds.

"Yeah, it was horrible," I said. "I mean, I knew I'd have to go but I thought I could wait until after class. But, man, then I got there and realized I was wrong. Way wrong. More wrong than a kid could ever be, you know?"

Mr. Gomez looked like he had no idea what to say to this. As his eyes darted around the hallway, I peeked at my watch again. Twenty-eight seconds.

"Anyway, so I was sitting there and I knew I couldn't hold it," I continued. "I tried crossing my legs, I tried thinking about sand, about the moon, about anything and everything but water. But then Zack, this kid who sits next to me and drinks way, way too much water, took out this massive jug of water and started drinking it. And I just, well, I lost control! I ran up to the teacher's desk, but she wouldn't let me go! And so then the urine just started . . ."

"Carson, I don't think this is appropriate. . . ." Mr. Gomez interrupted.

But I didn't give him a chance to finish. Because we were down to six seconds. I had to finish my story right now.

"And then, then it happened for real, right then and

there," I said, gradually raising my voice. "I mean, do you know what it's like? Can you know?!"

I was practically shouting now, and for just a split second between my words I heard Betsy talking inside my locker. So that's when I started pounding my fist on my locker door.

"Why me? Why me?! Why? Why? Why!?!?" I kept yelling and pounding. "Nobody will ever like me again! How can this happen?" I wailed in anguish.

Mr. Gomez stood next to me and raised and lowered his hands a few times in an awkward attempt to quiet me. I finally did stop yelling after I was sure that Betsy was done with her warning. Then I buried my face into my arm and pretended to sob quietly in shame as best I could.

"Um, okay, then, Carson. I'll, uh, I'll just leave you alone then," he said.

Good old Mr. Gomez. He was horrible at dealing with crying kids. He was pretty good at disciplining, and great at being a paranoid weirdo, but if any kid ever had a real-world problem like a parent dying or some other tragic thing, then Gomez would always clam up, start stammering, and flee as soon as he got the chance.

After Gomez retreated back to his office, I took my

backpack from my locker and checked my watch. Already just under thirteen minutes until the next warning. That meant it would go off twice during my first class. Could I really keep this up all day? I guess I would find out; I had no choice now. I didn't even have time to start thinking about how I would figure out which Mr. Jensen was the right one. This was turning into a much bigger ordeal than I had ever imagined.

The bell rang and kids poured out of their homerooms and flowed past me like a school of fish or something, totally unaware that they were encircling a device that could potentially save or destroy the whole country. A strange device that I had maybe compromised by bringing to school.

Like an idiot.

CHAPTER 10

THE KIDS AT MY SCHOOL MUST HAVE EITHER THOUGHT I WAS losing my mind that day or in the middle of some strange prank that would suddenly make sense by the end of it. For the next few classes, I carried my backpack with me. Which I know sounds stupid, but I couldn't risk leaving it alone anywhere. If it was with me at least I could control the situation. Well, that is if you can call yelling random stuff like a madman in the middle of class, or having twenty-three-second-long coughing fits every fifteen minutes controlling a situation.

Some kids laughed, but others were giving me weird looks. The same kids who probably never found my pranks funny. And also kids who didn't get that I was doing it on purpose, kids like Olek.

"You need neck lozenge?" he had asked after one of my particularly obnoxious coughing fits in fourth period.

It was hard not to laugh every time he spoke. Especially because he seemed like such a good guy, always so genuine and nice. It made his odd accent and poor English all the more hilarious for some reason. But in a good way. I wasn't actually laughing *at* him. There was something about the way he said things, a look in his eyes, that made me think he was in on the joke, that he knew his English was terrible and he was purposely playing it up to make me laugh.

"No, I'm good, Olek, thanks," I'd said.

"Your cough," he said, "is very American."

"What do you mean by that?" I asked.

"It is very loud."

"Well, I guess we just like to be noticed," I said.

"Huh" was his only reply. Then he turned away and seemed to ponder this response as if I'd just given the secret to the meaning of life. After a few moments he turned back. "Maybe this is why Jimmy Buffett is so good at music? To be heard over loud American coughs?"

I just shrugged. I was too preoccupied at this point to laugh at anything. Because I still had no idea which Mr. Jensen I needed to deliver Betsy to.

Like I said, there were two Mr. Jensens who taught at my school. To make things simple let's call them Tall Jensen and Short Jensen. Tall Jensen and Short Jensen are actually close to the same height. And neither one is particularly tall or short. Actually, they look pretty similar in general. Which is what makes this so confusing. Here's what I knew about both Mr. Jensens at my school:

Tall Jensen is a sixth-grade social studies teacher. I never had him for sixth grade, but my best friend Dillon did last year so I know a lot about him. Well, what Dillon actually told me was a whole bunch of stuff about Mr. Jensen secretly plotting to fail him, or how he was pretty sure Mr. Jensen was a vampire, or how a few weeks later he realized that of course Mr. Jensen wasn't a vampire, he was a vampire hunter, only to then admit that he was probably wrong about both of those things because Mr. Jensen was obviously a werewolf. He even tried to get me to sneak over to Tall Jensen's house with him one night when it was a full moon. Later that year, Dillon had recanted all of the monster stuff entirely and instead said he was pretty sure Tall Jensen was a master thief. He had to be since he was always sneaking around. Now, some might think that could be a clue that Tall Jensen was the right Jensen to deliver Betsy to, but the thing was, Dillon said something similar about almost every teacher he ever had.

Anyway, here's a summary of the real information that I was able to gather about Tall Jensen in between Dillon's crazy conspiracy theories:

- Tall Jensen had taught at our school for six years.
- He's around thirty years old.
- He drives a Nissan to work every day, except on Fridays for some reason, when he rides a bike (yes, there was a time when Dillon was following him to and from school to make sure he wasn't actually a troll who lived under the Eighth Street bridge).
- He's a fair but strict teacher, and his class could be pretty boring most of the time. But that's true for most classes.
- He's not married and does not have kids.
- He's the assistant coach of the eighth-grade

football team. He was definitely an athlete in high school and college, and still acts like most athletes do with the excessive manly posturing and spitting all over the place and high fives and all that.

- He's not a vampire or a vampire hunter or a werewolf, but he seems to be a fan of horror movies.

Based on all that, he didn't seem especially likely to be the Mr. Jensen that the dude in the suit had wanted me to deliver the package to. All signs pointed to him being a normal teacher.

But the real problem was that Short Jensen seemed even less likely.

Short Jensen was the school music teacher. I was in class with him two days a week last year and again this year. Here's what I knew about him:

- He teaches music, orchestra, and choir.
- He participates in the production of our school's annual plays and sometimes directs the musicals.
- He's married and has kids, and he talks about them in class a lot.

- He can often be heard humming softly when walking through the halls, or during downtime in class, or basically just all the time, really.
- He's also not a vampire, but unlike Tall Jensen, he does not like horror movies. In fact, one time in music class last year we watched this musical called *Phantom of the Opera*, which had exactly zero scary parts, but Short Jensen still had to turn away from the screen at least nine times because the movie was freaking him out. But, he had said afterward, "the splendid music necessitates showing the class this movie, despite its intense nature."

So my biggest dilemma was clearly trying to figure out how either one of these seemingly normal teachers could be the intended recipient of a strange device containing data so top secret that it would eventually self-destruct. I wondered briefly if maybe Betsy needed to be delivered to a totally different Mr. Jensen altogether, one who didn't even work for our school. One who worked somewhere in New York or LA or Washington, DC—places where cool spy stuff probably happens every day.

But I knew there was really only one way I could find

out for sure. I would need to talk to both Jensens. And I had a plan. Sort of. I was going to subtly drop some hints about the package into otherwise normal conversation. If one of them really was some sort of secret agent or spy, they'd undoubtedly pick up on it. I mean, what kind of secret agent would he be if he couldn't?

Since I was stuck in detention after school for the goat prank (another issue altogether since absolutely no talking was allowed in detention, especially not talking boxes or random shouting and loud, fake sneezing fits), it would be hard for me to find the time to track down either Mr. Jensen. But, unless I was planning on dooming the country by letting Betsy self-destruct with her information still locked inside, I would have to find a way.

010010110101000001010100101010010000
010101001001001010100101001010100101
0101000010010100101010010101010101010
000010101010101001100101010101010101
010101010100001010010101001010101010
010100001001010010101001010101010101010
00001010101010100110011010101
00101011010100010010
010100001001010010101

CHAPTER 11

IT WAS RIGHT AS FIFTH-PERIOD ENGLISH CLASS WAS STARTING
that I saw something suspicious.

Our teacher had just passed out a test. The class was
quiet as everyone got to work. I looked around the room
before starting on it myself. I watched kids' pencils wag-
ging in the air next to their heads in unison as they all
answered the same questions about some boring book
called *Great Expectations*. The very same questions a
bunch of students had answered the year before about
the same horrible book. And two years ago, and probably

even ten years ago. And they would be the same questions everybody would answer next year, too.

And the questions had never seemed more pointless to me. I mean, right now in my bag next to my desk was a device that apparently carried information vital to the safety of our whole country. And I was supposed to worry about some test on a book so boring I hadn't even made it past page four? I mean, hundreds of kids had probably failed this very same test over the past twenty-five years and what had happened to them because of it? Nothing, that's what. Now those kids were doing the same things that the kids who had passed the test were doing. Those kids were my parents' insurance agent, or the dude who drives the city bus, or an officer in the military, or the assistant manager at the Piggly Wiggly. Heck, maybe even one of my teachers. Because those are the things that pretty much all the kids from this town end up doing.

Anyway, the point is that I was watching everybody concentrate on the test instead of doing so myself, and that's why I saw the guys in suits through one of the classroom windows.

There were two of them, both wearing black business suits and sunglasses, snooping around in some bushes behind the school's western side. Even though there was no way they could see me through the heavily tinted school windows, I still had to resist the urge to dive down under my desk. They were looking in all the plants that surrounded the school, and talking to each other by speaking into the lapels of their jackets.

Unless they were severely overdressed landscapers, these guys—likely the same dudes who had kidnapped the package's courier—knew about the package and were still looking for it. Even if that wasn't the case, I had to assume it was. And the fact that they were here meant they must have figured out that the guy had either stashed it somewhere on school property or given it to some kid or teacher.

The thing I couldn't figure out, and have never really understood, is why spies and secret agents and other such dudes in movies always wear suits and sunglasses. They're clearly trying to blend in, be inconspicuous, but everyone has seen those same movies, so really there's no better way to look suspicious or stand out than to a wear a black suit and black tie and black sunglasses, right?

The two guys crawling around behind the bushes looked about as natural back there as Sasquatch would look sunbathing on a Hawaiian beach. But their black sunglasses were impenetrable, and they gave me the creeps. Especially because I knew that I had exactly what they were looking for.

"What are you looking at?" Danielle whispered to me. "You've been staring out the window for ten straight minutes."

I turned and looked at her. I honestly had kind of forgotten that I was supposed to be taking a test right now. Thankfully our teacher was always reading some book while we took tests and barely noticed what any of us did as long as we weren't starting fires or inciting riots or something like that.

"I was just . . ." I began as I turned back to the window. But the two guys in suits were gone. Or at least weren't visible from my seat anymore. "Never mind, I'm just tired today."

"Yeah, I guess," she said skeptically. "I heard about your, uh, *issues* this morning in homeroom."

I grinned and shrugged. "Hey, duty calls."

"Gross," she said, but I could tell she was holding back a laugh.

That was why Danielle was the coolest girl I'd ever met. She found stuff funny that would make a lot of girls roll their eyes or want to barf or something. But I guess that all made sense considering that she was Dillon's twin sister. You had to have a pretty good sense of humor to deal with that kid your whole life.

"I won't be there at lunch today," I whispered. "Let everyone know I'm sorry."

Danielle, Dillon, and I sat at the same lunch table every day with a few of our other friends. But today I couldn't make it because I was planning to use that time to see if I could track down Short Jensen.

"That's too bad. We were all going to celebrate how hilarious school has been today, watching teachers struggle with all the stuff glued to their desks. What exactly are you up to anyway? Dillon told me you were acting all weird and secretive this morning, and Zack said you took your backpack to the bathroom with you during third period. Got some prank that we can't be in on for some reason?"

"Maybe. I guess you'll just have to wait and see."

I glanced at my watch. Betsy's next announcement would be in just a few minutes, which meant I'd need to get out of there pretty soon. I'd likely just ask to leave to use the bathroom this time around, since shouting in the middle of a test was probably not a great idea. Even though most of the class looked to be finished by now.

Well, except for me, that is.

"Look, I gotta go to the bathroom, sorry," I said, quickly filling in a bunch of random answers on the multiple-choice test.

"Well, if you won't be at lunch, can we all hang out tonight or something?" Danielle asked.

I was about to say yeah when I suddenly thought of us all hanging out with Betsy there, too, announcing every fifteen minutes that she was going to self-destruct.

"I can't tonight," I said. "Tomorrow night, though, for sure. I swear."

I got up, grabbed my bag and test, and went up front to turn in my guaranteed F and ask the teacher if I could use the bathroom. Just before I left the room, I glanced out the window and saw the two guys in suits talking to the janitor in the parking lot. As they talked to him, their heads turned from side to side. Clearly looking for something.

Me.

And the package.

1010010110101000001010100101010010101001010010000
10101010010010010101010010101001010101001010101001
01010100001001010010101010010101010101010
0000101010101010100110010101010101010101
010101010101000010100101010100101010101010
0101010000100101001010101001011010101010
00001010101010101001100110101
01010110101000100100
0010101001001001010101
CHAPTER 12

I WASN'T ACTUALLY SURE WHETHER OR NOT I'D BE ABLE TO FIND Short Jensen during lunch. I'd only had him two days a week the last two years for required general music class, so I had no idea what he did during lunch every day. Did he eat in the cafeteria? In the teachers' lounge? At some restaurant nearby? Did he not eat food at all because he really was a cyborg like Dillon had once claimed last year?

I didn't know. But I figured the best place to start was his classroom.

As I walked there against the flow of kids heading to lunch, I checked my watch. Only a few seconds left until Betsy's next update. I took a few deep breaths and then started singing the modified school song at the top of my lungs. I got a few grins and smirks and even some chuckles as I passed kids. But for the first time, a few kids actually looked a little annoyed. I guess the random shouting and singing was funny only so many times. But that wasn't really my concern right then.

When I got to the music room, the lights were off. I debated going to the teachers' lounge to see if Short Jensen was in there, but the more I thought about that idea, the dumber it seemed. How could I "casually hint" at anything when I'd invaded the teachers' lounge during their lunch break?

No, that wouldn't work.

My only option was to sit outside his room and wait. It might make me late for my sixth-period class, but I had no other choice. Betsy's counter was going to hit zero in, like, thirty hours, and I only had so many chances to talk to the two Jensens before then. I sat on the floor next to his door and waited. Luckily no one was around to hear Betsy give her next warning, so I didn't even try to cover it up.

"You now have thirty-three hours to initiate fail-safe measures before self-destruction."

The minutes ticked by. Betsey gave another warning. I was sweating pretty hard at this point, even though I hadn't moved in twenty minutes. Finally, with only about six minutes left of my lunch period, Short Jensen showed up.

I sprang to my feet.

"Hey," he said, pausing as he clearly struggled to remember my name. "Carson, what's going on?"

"Not much, Mr. Jensen," I said. "I just need to talk to you, if that's okay?"

The look on his face turned into a smile and he opened his classroom door.

"Sure, come on in."

My mind was racing. Just what exactly was I going to say to him? It had all seemed so much easier in my head earlier. *Yeah, I'll just see Short Jensen, and then, despite the fact that I haven't talked to him one-on-one pretty much ever, I'll have an easy and casual conversation with him about any number of topics, during which I'll drop in some sly hints about a secret package containing top secret information so important that it will self-destruct in less than two days. And he'll definitely pick up on those subtle hints, because he's likely a highly trained secret agent of some sort.*

Playing it back in my head, now of course it seemed as ridiculous of a plan as it really was.

"So," Short Jensen said as he sat down behind his small desk, "what's on your mind?"

"Well, I was thinking about maybe auditioning for the school musical."

I honestly had no idea where that had come from. It just sort of fell out when I opened my mouth. I definitely had no interest in the school's next musical, but I had to admit it was at least a believable reason for me to be there. And it's not like asking about it meant I actually had to audition or anything.

"That's great, Carson! I admit that I'm a little surprised since you've never shown any interest before, but just the same, that's fantastic."

I nodded. I suppose if I were actually interested in the musical, that would be fantastic from his perspective. Or maybe he just said stuff like that to everyone who showed interest in theater.

"We're going to try to tackle *Sweeney Todd* this year, if you can believe that."

"Oh, uh, wow, that's cool," I said even though I

obviously had no idea what *Sweeney Todd* was. "So, when are the auditions?"

"Next Thursday at 3:45."

Okay, this was going well enough, but I still hadn't managed to drop any hints.

"Do I need to bring anything?"

He frowned. "No . . . why do you ask?"

"Well, I just thought maybe I needed to bring a certain prop or something to help me get a part. Like a bag of squirrels, if I was going to be a crazy, squirrel-collecting hobo. Or maybe like a certain self-destructing computer if I was auditioning for the part of someone who had to deliver sensitive information to a secret agent or something."

When I said this I tried to give him my most meaningful look. A look that conveyed that there was more to what I'd just said than you'd expect. And at first I thought it had worked, because Short Jensen didn't say anything for at least five seconds.

He just sat there and stared at me, as if he was still trying to process what he'd just heard.

"You haven't actually ever heard of *Sweeney Todd*, have you, Carson?"

I shook my head.

"Are you trying to get in the play so you can pull some sort of prank during the show? Is that what this is?"

He didn't seem mad, necessarily, but he did seem a little disappointed. And maybe even a little amused, too. I didn't know what to say back.

"The teachers know, Carson. Well, most of us do, anyway. About your . . . extracurricular activities."

"I don't know what you're talking about," I said.

"Will that be all?" he asked.

He was clearly done with this conversation. There was no way it could be Short Jensen. The hint I'd dropped had been about as subtle as an anvil to the face, and his only reaction had been to assume I was planning to sabotage his play.

"Yeah, that's all," I said, and turned to leave.

"So should I expect to see you at the audition next week?" he asked as I got to the door.

I stopped. I debated lying, but what would really be the point now? I turned back.

"No, probably not."

He smiled.

"That's too bad," he said.

Well, he had been right about me lying regarding the audition. But he couldn't have been more wrong when it came to why I'd lied. I actually sort of wished his reason was the truth. I really did. As exciting as all this had been at first, now I was actually getting worried I would be stuck with Betsy right up until the end of her countdown, and then whatever vital information she carried would be destroyed, and it would all be my fault.

1001011010101000001010100101010100100000
010101001001001010101001010010101001010
010100001001010010101010010101010101010101
000101010101010100110010101010101010101010
0101010101010000010100101010010101010100
010100001001010010101010010101010101010101
00001   0011001010101010101010
0010   0010101010010101010101
01   10101010010101010101010101
0   11010101010101010101

CHAPTER 13

THE GOOD NEWS REGARDING MY MEETING WITH SHORT JENSEN was that if he wasn't the Mr. Jensen I was looking for, then it had to be Tall Jensen. I'll admit I even debated just dropping Betsy on his desk after school that day. But then I thought about the guy in the suit, about how desperate he had been. The pasty-faced guys who captured him, the car that drove past my house last night, the guys searching through the bushes outside the school today. Whatever this thing was, it was important. Too important to just abandon on some random teacher's desk without knowing for sure.

The bad news was that I was late for my next class and earned another hour's worth of detention. I could never join any sport or after-school club even if I'd wanted to because I'd logged enough detention around this place to already have an after-school activity taking up my time.

"So, where were you at lunch today?" Dillon asked when I walked into sixth-period life sciences. "Danielle said you were acting all secretive and strange again last hour."

"I just had some stuff to do, that's all. Why are you being so nosy?"

"Why are you acting so suspiciously?"

I shook my head and was about to come up with some lie when Ms. Greenwood stepped in between our desks.

"Is there something I should know about?" she asked. "You're insisting on talking in my class. So I assume there must be something important happening back here."

For a moment, I thought she might be talking about Betsy. But how could she know?

"No, sorry, Ms. Greenwood," Dillon said. "We'll be quiet."

She paused for a moment, staring at me for what I thought was at least five seconds too long. Then she gave

Dillon that same *I mean it* look and walked back toward the front of the classroom.

"See? I told you she has super-subsonic hearing!" he whispered while her footsteps covered his voice. "She's definitely a bionic superwoman constructed by the government. The way you were just staring at Ms. Greenwood, I could tell you know I'm right this time. You looked as if she could read your mind, which, you know, she totally can. I've been saying it all year. . . ."

I stared at him for a moment, then shook my head and forced a smile. What was wrong with me? I was so paranoid I was practically turning into Dillon myself! Of course she couldn't have known about Betsy.

Ms. Greenwood shot us another look from the front of the room and then went back to talking about photosynthesis. Just a few minutes later, a folded piece of paper landed on my desk. I looked at Dillon and he nodded his head at me. The good old-fashioned note system.

I opened the folded slip of notebook paper and read the message:

I KNOW WHATS IN YOUR BACKPACK.

How could he possibly know? I looked over at Dillon, and he was sitting there nodding at me smugly. I shook my head like I didn't know what he was talking about. He wrote something else on another slip of paper, looked up front to make sure Ms. Greenwood wasn't looking, and then passed it to me.

ITS A SELF-DESTRUCTING SECRET MESSAGE ISNT IT?

I flipped the paper over and wrote furiously on the back.

Don't be stupid! Why do you think that?

I passed the paper back to Dillon when I was sure Ms. Greenwood wasn't looking. He looked at my message and then smirked. It was almost triumphant. He wrote a new message down, a long one, and passed it back.

BECAUSE I SWORE I HEARD IT SAY IT WOULD SELF-DESTRUCT THIS MORNING PLUS YER OBVIOUSLY HIDING SOMETHING IN THERE!!!! WHATS IT FOR? ARE THEY AFTER YOU?

I flipped his note over and wrote another reply.

Are you crazy?!?! Why would I bring something like that to school? I'm not that stupid.

Of course the irony was that I was indeed that stupid. Dillon read the note, and then scribbled his reply and passed it back.

I NEVER DID THINK IT WAS THAT ANYWAY. I'M

ACTUALLY PRETTY SURE IT'S A GREMLIN. YOU
GOT A GREMLIN SOMEHOW DIDN'T YOU? I KNEW
IT!!!!!!!!

If class were long enough, we would have gone back
and forth for hours with Dillon moving from one theory
to another. Either way, I was relieved that Dillon was just
being Dillon and really hadn't figured out what I had in
my backpack.

A few times during our exchange, though, I saw the
same two guys wearing suits outside again. They were
going from car to car in the school parking lot, looking
inside the windows. A shiver went up my spine. They
were relentless.

What exactly was in this box that was so important?

0100101101010100000101010010101001010000
0101010010010010101010010100101010100101
1010100001001010010101010010101010101010
0001010101010101001100101010101010101010
0101010101010000101001010100101010100101
1010100001001010010101001010101010101010
0001010101010100110010000 ⬤ 01010
00101011010100010010 ⬤ 0100
10101000010010100010 CHAPTER 14 010

CHAPTER 14

FINDING TALL JENSEN WAS A LOT EASIER THAN FINDING SHORT Jensen. For one, I knew exactly where he'd be after school. Being the assistant football coach meant he was at football practice every day until at least 5:00 p.m. Which was good for me, since I didn't get out of detention until 4:15.

Detention was a whole other nightmare altogether. I mean, no talking is allowed in detention. At all. So I had to do something with Betsy if I didn't want to get found out.

I debated storing her inside the evergreen tree right outside the detention room window where I could keep an eye on her, but with those two goons in suits nosing around all day, that didn't seem like a particularly smart idea either.

Stashing her in my locker was also definitely out, as there were sometimes even more kids wandering the halls after school than during school. Especially from 3:00 until 3:45 while they were waiting for rides, chatting with friends, and going to and from their various extracurricular activities and clubs.

I also couldn't just skip detention. I know that seems silly since this Betsy mess was potentially a major national security threat. But I'd skipped detention before, and Gomez had made it very clear that if I did it again, I'd be suspended for sure, maybe even expelled.

So where did that leave me?

Well, it left me with the only thing I could possibly think of: asking Dillon and Danielle for help.

I didn't really want to drag them into this, but I had nowhere else to turn. Plus, I trusted them. Dillon was too crazy to be untrustworthy, as strange as that sounds, and Danielle was likely the person I trusted the most outside of my family. Whereas I hated responsibilities and chores and all that crap, Danielle thrived on it. She loved school projects and couldn't wait to turn fifteen so she could get a job, if you can actually believe that. She *liked* tasks. Her life's goal was to be president of the United States. No joke. One time when she and Dillon were at my house, she reorganized my entire game closet because she got so mad when I couldn't find the board game we wanted to play. After she left that day, my brother had said, "You need to have an intervention for your friend Danielle. That girl is literally addicted to *accomplishments*."

Anyway, the point is that I could trust them. Besides, I didn't need to tell them everything. Dillon had a pretty open mind, so I could make up pretty much anything I wanted and keep him on a strict need-to-know basis, and Danielle always assumed half the stuff I said was exaggerated or made up, so I could probably just tell her the truth and she wouldn't even believe me anyway. It wasn't that I lied all the time or anything. I think she was like that as a byproduct of having Dillon for a twin brother.

After school, I went to the west entrance, where they always met each day to wait for their mom to pick them up.

"Hey, need a ride today, Carson?" Dillon asked as I approached.

I usually rode the bus home, but from time to time, on the rare days I didn't have detention, I would catch a ride with them.

"Of course he doesn't!" Danielle corrected him in that way that sisters love to do. "He has detention today, remember? Don't you actually need to be there right now?"

"Yeah, that's actually why I came to see you. I need your help."

"See?" Dillon said, smacking his sister's arm lightly, "I told you he was in trouble with spies! What did you do, steal some super–top secret plans?"

"Shut up already about the spies!" Danielle said, smacking him back but much harder. Then she turned to me. "He's got some stupid theory about spies snooping around the school as a part of some international espionage conspiracy just because he saw some guy in a suit in the parking lot today. I mean, jeez, it's not like every guy wearing a suit is a spy. Besides this is *North Dakota.*"

I was glad that Danielle had spoken up so quickly, because otherwise I don't think I could have hidden my shock at what Dillon had just said. Sometimes I had to wonder if there were some things Dillon said that he just might be right about. Like, for instance, the last thing he'd just said.

"Yeah, no kidding," I said. "Jeez, Dillon."

"Whatever, you'll see someday," Dillon said, like he always did.

"Anyway, guys," I said, "the thing is, Dillon isn't that far off. You see, I was working on this new prank. It was going to involve me tricking Gomez into thinking he was caught up in some sort of spy conspiracy."

"Cool!" Dillon said.

"Go on," Danielle said.

They both loved messing with Gomez as much as I did. He was just so high-strung; it always made our pranks especially fun when he was the target.

"Anyway," I continued, "I made this fake self-destructing message device. But apparently I haven't worked out all the kinks yet because it won't stop talking. It announces that it's going to self-destruct every fifteen minutes."

"At least that explains why you've been acting so strange," Danielle said. "Let me guess, you want us to take your bag and take it somewhere where people won't hear it while you're in detention, right?"

I smiled and nodded and gave them my best *pretty-please* look.

"Okay, fine," she said.

"I'm not taking that thing!" Dillon said, stepping back.

"Dillon, it's not *real*," I lied. "It's perfectly harmless. I made it using some old computer that I bought on eBay for twenty bucks."

"Yeah, well, that's probably exactly what someone with a real self-destructing secret message would say."

"Don't mind him," Danielle said. "I'll take it for you. But you owe me!" She loved doing favors for people, mostly because she loved it when people owed her favors. *Favors are the world's most valuable currency*, she once told me. *Nobody does anything that matters all on their own.*

"Where are we gonna take it, and what about mom?" Dillon said. "She'll think we were kidnapped by a gang of Elvis impersonators if we're not here."

I laughed, but Danielle rolled her eyes as she took the bag from me.

"We'll just text her and tell her we don't need a ride until later since we're hanging out with Carson after school today," Danielle said. "I think I know the perfect spot to bring this."

"Behind the sledding hill is where I was thinking," I said.

Our school was built on a big hill, basically, and one side was a particularly popular sledding spot in the winter. The hill was so steep that there was one area off to the side that was like a dirt cliff with a ton of holes in it where a bunch of swallows had made their nests. It was a pretty isolated spot when there was no snow on the ground, and kids hardly ever went down there. We usually didn't either; there was something about it that just never felt right, so we all avoided it. It was hard to explain. But the point is, it would be the perfect hiding spot for Betsy.

"Exactly," Danielle said. "Me, too. How much time before it talks again?"

I checked my watch and then looked up.

"Ninety seconds. You guys better run. I'll meet you there after detention."

Danielle nodded and grabbed Dillon's arm, and then they took off running toward the sledding hill.

"Thanks!" I yelled after them before hustling to detention myself. The detention supervisor hated tardiness—I guess because that's exactly why most kids got detention in the first place.

0100101101010100000101010100101010010010100100110
010101001001001001010100100101001001010100100101010
1010100001001010010101010010010101010101010101010
00001010101010101001100101010101010101010101010
010101010101000001010010101010010101010100
10101000010010100101010100101010101010101
00001⬤   ⬤0011001010101010101010101010
001⬤   ⬤00101010100101010100101
101   1010100101010101010101

CHAPTER 15

LATER, AFTER DETENTION BUT BEFORE MEETING BACK UP WITH Dillon and Danielle, I went to the practice football field to talk to Tall Jensen.

I made my way there with slow plodding steps to buy some thinking time. I faced the same problem I had earlier with Short Jensen: What reason would I have for needing to talk to Tall Jensen? Especially seeing as how I'd never even had Tall Jensen as a teacher? At least I knew that this time I likely had the right guy. There weren't any Jensens left at the school, unless the guy in the suit had been talking about Lisa Jensen. But a sixth-grade girl obsessed with horses and *American Idol* was even less likely to be a secret agent than Short Jensen.

When I got to the football field, I saw Tall Jensen standing on one of those giant football pads on a platform with springs behind it. Sleds, I think the football players call them. He yelled at a group of six or seven players. Then he blew his whistle, and one of the kids sprang out of his stance and into the pad. It barely even moved.

"Pathetic!" Tall Jensen shouted. "Next!"

He blew his whistle again, and the next kid tried. When he hit the pad, instead of the pad moving back on its springs, the kid bounced off it and fell back onto his butt like the pad was made of bouncy-ball rubber.

Tall Jensen shook his head in defeat. "That's it, ladies, give me three laps around the goalposts, end to end." The players groaned in unison and started jogging toward the nearest goalpost.

I approached Tall Jensen, still not entirely sure what I was going to say.

"Can I help you?" he asked.

"Oh, I just wanted to check out practice," I said. "See what it's like. I might try out next year."

Tall Jensen nodded and turned his head to watch the

seven players he'd been yelling at run the first lap. Some of the other players, who were in several groups with a few other coaches, pointed and laughed at their teammates as they ran by.

"Yeah, well, I'm sorry you had to see that," he said.

I shrugged.

"What position?"

"Huh?" I said.

"If you played, what position do you think you'd like?" Tall Jensen looked at me from head to toe.

I'd never really thought about that before. I wasn't really into sports that much. I mean, I used to play pretty much all of them when I was little because that's what all little kids do around here, but none of them quite stuck once I got older. Spending my free time planning pranks was always more fun and exciting to me than winning some pointless game that tens of millions of other kids were also winning or losing all across the country. In fact, I only knew the names of a few positions in football.

"Uh, quarterback, I guess," I said.

Tall Jensen laughed and shook his head.

"That's what they all say. Which is funny since only one kid can play that position. You don't look like a quarterback, though—I'll say that much. Maybe a cornerback."

I didn't really know what a cornerback was, but I suddenly had this image of me wearing football equipment and huddling in a corner somewhere.

"Well, people don't always look like what they actually are," I said. "Like, say, teachers. Sometimes teachers actually look like teachers, and other times they look like secret agents or spies only posing as teachers. Or vice versa. You know what I mean?"

Tall Jensen squinted at me and then picked something out of his ear, before obnoxiously hawking up a loogie and spitting it into the grass near his feet.

Gross.

"What are you talking about, kid?" he said.

The way he'd been looking at me had changed. Instead of looking at me as a potential cornerback, now he was looking at me like he might want to refer me to the state mental institution in Jamestown.

"I just meant that sometimes people aren't what they seem," I said.

"Yeah," he said slowly.

Then we just looked at each other for a moment. A sort of uncomfortable silence passed, during which I debated how to bring up the package specifically.

"Yeah," he said again. "Maybe you are more of a wide

receiver type. Can you catch?"

I nodded.

He walked over to a mesh bag with some footballs in it and took one out. He gave me a single head nod and then threw it at me. I caught it pretty easily. Just because I wasn't into sports didn't mean I wasn't coordinated enough to catch a ball.

He held up his hands for me to throw it back.

I hesitated. Throwing a football was another matter entirely. It was something I hadn't really done much outside of gym class. I gripped it like I remembered and threw. It came out of my hand like a duck missing both a wing and a brain. Still, it floated its way close enough to Tall Jensen for him to jog a few steps and make the catch.

"You want to be a quarterback?" he said, raising an eyebrow.

"Yeah, well, I guess I just like to deliver stuff. You know, footballs, pizzas, secret packages with sensitive information, whatever," I said. "You know of any other way I can deliver something to someone in school other than to play quarterback?"

Again there was a pause before he responded. It probably was taking his brain extra long to digest the weird things I was saying. Pretty soon I was going to get a different reputation than a prankster. I might start to be known as the crazy kid that people say likes to catch beetles and eat them with mayonnaise or something.

"You're really a weird kid. I know as a teacher I'm not supposed to say that, but . . ." Mr. Jensen finally said, finishing with a shrug.

All right. So it wasn't this Jensen either. I guess I wasn't sure exactly what I'd expected him to say or do, but I had been so convinced that this was the right Jensen that I hadn't thought much about what I'd do if he showed no reaction to my clues. His players were finally getting back from their laps, breathing hard.

Tall Jensen blew his whistle and started screaming at the few lagging behind to hustle. And with that, our conversation was over. And so were my chances of unloading Betsy today. I sighed and headed toward the sledding hill.

Danielle was sitting against a tree with my bag in her lap. Dillon was standing near the swallow nest holes, gazing up at them vacantly.

"What's his deal?" I asked as Danielle stood up and handed me my bag.

103

"He thinks he sees tiny cameras or something inside the swallow nests." She shook her head and rolled her eyes.

Dillon must have heard us talking because he turned around suddenly, looking pretty spooked.

"I heard a lens motor, I swear. They're watching us."

"Who are *they* this time?" I asked.

He shrugged.

"Could be anybody, really. But I'm convinced it's likely the government in some form. I mean, who else would waste money putting tiny cameras in swallow nests that overlook nothing but the water treatment plant across the street and that shed in the grove of trees over there? Unless there's something secret happening here? Like weird experiments on kids' brains. You guys ever see that old movie *Disturbing Behavior*?"

Dillon watched a ton of movies. His favorites were horror, science fiction, and of course psychological thrillers with ridiculous plot twists and corrupt senators and all that stuff. Pretty much any movies with secrets, double-crosses, and inane plot twists were right up his alley. They're probably part of what fueled his own conspiracy theories.

"Yeah, you made us watch it with you, remember?" Danielle said.

"Oh, yeah." Dillon finally peeled himself away from the swallow nests. He stole a few last distrustful glances back as he walked toward us.

"Any problems with the device?" I asked.

Danielle shook her head. "No, but I almost took it out and smashed it to pieces several times because it got so annoying listening to Dolores talk about fail-safe measures every fifteen minutes."

"Oh, well it's good you didn't. Ha-ha," I said. My heart raced. What if she had? Would it have self-destructed right then and there? Had I been that close to inadvertently causing harm to my two best friends, not to mention the whole country?

"Why did you say that? I thought it wasn't real?" Danielle asked.

"No, it's not. I just need to return some of the parts where I bought them. Can't do that if they're smashed, right?"

She nodded.

"You named it Dolores?" I asked.

She grinned.

"I've been calling her Betsy," I said.

"Like after Betsy Hummel, that passive-aggressive brat in our math class?" Danielle said.

"That's the one," I said.

Dillon scoffed. "You're both terrible at naming stuff. Those are, like, cows' names or something. I'd have called her Isis."

"Want to come over?" Danielle asked.

"No, I have to take care of this thing first. See if I can get it to shut up. Maybe tomorrow?"

"How about a ride then? You've missed the late bus by now," Danielle said. "My mom is on her way."

"How would I explain Betsy to her?" I asked.

"You mean Isis?" Dillon said.

"Good point," Danielle said, ignoring her brother's remark. "Okay, see you tomorrow at lunch then. Let's get out of here, this area gives me the creeps for some reason."

"Yeah, sounds good," I said. We headed our separate ways.

01001011101010100000101010010101010100100000
101010100100100100101010010100010101010010 1
010101000001001010010101010010101010101010
000010101010101010011001010101010101010101
001010101010100000101001010101001010101010
010101000010010100101010010101010101010
000010101010101010011001   0101
00101011010100010010   0100
0101000010010100101   010
0 0 0   0 1

THE CREEPY DARK SEDAN WITH NO HEADLIGHTS DROVE DOWN my street again that night. I didn't see how they could know that I had the package, but at the same time I didn't know if I could afford to assume that they were just driving up and down random streets in town. Either way, it was still terrifying to see them creeping past my house.

Not that it really mattered anymore. As Betsy had warned me after dinner, I only had twenty-three hours until she self-destructed. And I still had no idea who the package needed to be delivered to. There was no way I was just going to leave it somewhere random either. If it really did contain information that the country depended on, I couldn't have it on my conscience to just let it self-destruct.

I spent most of that night lying in bed replaying my conversations with the two Jensens over and over again. Trying to see if there was some look or signal that I'd missed. Something that would give me some hope that one of them was the intended recipient of the package.

But it was sort of hard because I'd gotten a lot of weird looks from both of them. From their perspectives I must have sounded crazy. Maybe I was crazy? Maybe this thing was still a hoax after all? Some hugely elaborate prank orchestrated by Dillon and Danielle?

It was this surprisingly disappointing idea that finally put me to sleep. I mean, if that was actually the truth, then it should have made me happy because then the pressure of having the fate of the country in my hands would be off my shoulders. But it also would mean that things would go back to normal.

But it didn't matter. Reality woke me the next morning in the form of Betsy's voice.

"You now have twelve hours and forty-five minutes to initiate fail-safe measures before self-destruction."

As I was brushing my teeth that morning, I decided I just needed to take action. I simply couldn't be in possession of Betsy when her countdown hit zero. I couldn't be responsible for failing to carry out one little task and bringing doom to the whole country. I would have to just pick the most likely Jensen and give Betsy to him. That would be that. And even if that meant I'd have to go back to days so predictable that I could almost write them out every morning before they even happened, well, then so be it.

I synched my watch to the timer like the day before, put Betsy in my bag like the day before, and then got on the bus to go to school like the day before. The difference was this time I would not be coming home with the device still in my bag.

Olek sat next to me on the bus again. I didn't even consider stopping him. I kind of liked him, despite the fact that he always smelled like dry milk and cardboard. He made me laugh, and a good laugh here or there is just what a guy needs sometimes.

"Ah, hello, you again," he said, sitting down.

"Hey, Olek," I said.

"Ah!" he yelled. "You say my name right!"

I smiled and nodded. There weren't exactly a lot of

foreign people in North Dakota, and so the few who did live here had their names mispronounced constantly. I had a teacher once who kept calling Jesus (pronounced *Hey-Seuss*) *Jeez-us* all year long even though he corrected her every time she said it wrong during that first month. Eventually, he just gave up. But that's North Dakota for you. I mean, Jesus isn't even a hard name to say.

I peeked at my watch. Seven minutes until the next warning.

"You sing song again?" Olek asked.

"Actually, yes."

"Good, I help you," he said. "Only, I sing song from my country."

"A Jimmy Buffett song?"

"Yes, of course! You hear how magical his songs are. Like unicorn horn!"

"Awesome, thanks!" I managed to say while laughing. "Yeah, sing it as loud as you can."

"Now?"

"I'll tell you when," I said.

Olek nodded and grinned even wider. I was really starting to like this kid. If this whole package situation didn't result in my arrest or the collapse of the whole country, I was thinking it wouldn't be so bad to hang out with him more often. Kind of like Dillon, I could see him bringing something unexpected to each day. Although, to be fair, I'd gotten so used to Dillon's theories that even those seemed like a predictable routine these days.

"Want see something cool?" Olek asked.

"Sure," I said.

He opened his backpack and showed me an old black boot. It was like a work boot with a steel toe. It was dirty and old.

"What is that?" I asked.

"You never see shoe before?" he asked.

"No, I just . . . I mean, why is it in your bag, Olek?"

"I find it outside in street today. Crazy, yeah? I mean, who throw away perfectly good shoe!"

"I don't know that I would call it *perfectly* good," I said.

"Why, what wrong with it? Has it some defect that I not see?" He inspected the boot closely, turning it over in his hands.

I laughed and then he grinned at me but continued to examine the boot.

"Please, show me where defect exists," he said, holding out the old boot.

"I was kidding. It's a perfectly good boot," I said.

"Yes, this what I think also. In my country, this find

does not exist. Nobody throw away perfectly good shoe. But here, what they say, some man's old trash can contain some other man's money satchel?"

"You mean, one man's trash is another man's treasure?" I offered.

"Yes, this what I say," Olek said.

I checked my watch. I'd almost forgotten.

"Anyway, are you ready to sing?" I said.

Olek nodded.

"Okay, start singing in three, two, one . . ."

CHAPTER 17

WHEN WE GOT TO SCHOOL THAT MORNING, I SAW TALL JENSEN with a football tucked under one arm standing by the front entrance. It had to be a sign. I mean, it was pretty unusual. He'd never before been assigned morning door-monitoring duty since I'd started going to school here last year. Then I was even more surprised when he held up the football and motioned toward me with it.

I gave him a questioning look and he waved me over. This was about more than just him wanting to say hi to me randomly or something. This had to be about Betsy.

"Hey," I said as I walked up to him.

"Just the guy I wanted to see," he said.

"Really?"

He nodded. "Look, I owe you an apology. I probably shouldn't have called you weird like I did yesterday. That was uncalled for."

"It's okay, Mr. Jensen," I said. "I *was* acting a little weird."

"Listen, what I mean to say is that if you want to try out for the team next year, then by all means go for it. Even if you want to be quarterback because you like to deliver stuff or whatever, I shouldn't discourage you. That is, whatever reason you have for wanting to try out for the team is okay. It doesn't matter. Even if you end up being terrible, we can always use more bodies for the starters to knock around in practice."

"Oh, okay," I said.

"That was a joke," he said.

"Yeah, I know," I said. "Well, thanks, Mr. Jensen. I'll keep that in mind next year."

"All right, good deal. Have a nice day, Carson," he said.

"Uh, thanks," I said, and walked past him and into the school.

That was it. It had to be. That was his signal to me

that he was the guy I was looking for after all. There was no other explanation. I mean, from what I knew of him, Tall Jensen wasn't exactly the sort of guy who tracked down kids to make apologies for something so insignificant. All he'd done the day before is call me out when I'd acted like a complete weirdo.

So that's why, right after I entered the building, before I even went to my locker, I made a quick stop at Tall Jensen's classroom. His door was open and the lights were on, but the room was empty. I knew that he'd show up before too long, though. After the buses all made their drop-offs, he'd leave the front door and make a quick pit stop at the teachers' lounge before heading back here to his classroom. Teachers always made stops at the teachers' lounge whenever they could, probably to get coffee or cry or fistfight one another or do who knows what. But that didn't matter. What mattered was that he'd be back shortly and that meant I could just ditch Betsy here and now and take off without having to explain anything further.

I took Betsy out of my bag and put it on his desk. I turned to leave but then considered that some of his students might show up before he got here. They might get curious as to what the strange black box on their teacher's desk was. So I went back and moved Betsy to his chair, which I then pushed all the way in to the desk.

As I was walking away, I heard Betsy's voice for what I hoped would be the last time:

"You now have ten hours to initiate fail-safe measures before self-destruction."

I basically sprinted out of his classroom and to my locker. And then it was suddenly over.

Just like that.

And even though I was relieved to finally get rid of Betsy, part of me was sort of bummed that it was all over. I mean, for the past day I had been involved in some crazy spy plot. For real! And now, things were suddenly back to normal.

Compared to the last few days, the rest of that day was about as boring as you can get. Well, except for at lunch when Dillon tried to convince us that bananas were actually extinct. He said that real bananas went extinct in the 1950s and the ones we've all been eating were genetically manufactured replicas or something. He also said that they were putting stuff in the bananas that made people fart because they don't want banana lovers to be able to breed easily.

"What?" Danielle shouted.

"Yeah, that's a stretch even for you," I said. "Who's the 'they' this time, anyway?"

"The 1988 Olympic US hockey team," he said. "Obviously."

I'd laughed so hard that I almost choked on a green bean.

Even detention felt extra boring later that day. It's never terrible; it's not exactly torture or anything. But it was always pretty boring. You weren't allowed to read or play games on your phone or anything like that. You were given two options: (1) do homework or (2) sit there quietly. But now it felt even more boring than usual, knowing that there wasn't a top secret package that I needed to covertly deliver to a spy afterward.

By the time detention ended there usually weren't too many kids left wandering the halls because after-school activities were either over or still going on in some room or practice field somewhere. I got my backpack from my locker and then headed out the side entrance, hoping to be able to catch the late bus home so I wouldn't have to walk.

It left usually within a few minutes of detention ending, so some days I caught it and some days I didn't. I rounded the corner that day just in time to see it pulling away from the curb, its double exhaust pipes blasting gray fumes behind it as if to rub it in my face.

I sighed and walked back around behind the school, the shortest route to my house. I'd only just turned off school property when I saw the men with suits standing on the sidewalk, right in my path.

There were two of them. Black suits, black ties, black sunglasses.

"Howdy," one of them said.

Howdy? Where did he think we were, Deadwood?

"Hey," I said and kept walking toward them, pretending that there was nothing at all unusual about two guys wearing suits standing outside of a school in Middle-of-Nowhere, North Dakota.

"You seen a kid around here?" the other guy asked.

I was only a few feet away now and I saw that their faces were both glistening with sweat. As if they'd been standing outside in the sun all day. There was something familiar about them, even as generic as they looked.

"Yeah," I said. "Lots of them. It's a school."

The one on my left clenched his fists by his sides. The one on the right crouched down so he was at my level and then took off his sunglasses. As soon as he did, I realized why he'd looked so familiar. He was one of the guys I'd seen abducting the dude who had given me the package. I hadn't recognized him because his face wasn't nearly as pasty as it had been on that day. But I recognized his eyes immediately. This was the same guy who I could've sworn had looked right at me before they all piled into the unmarked sedan and drove off.

"We're looking for one particular kid," he said. "He's probably about this tall and has dark hair."

He held his hand in the air to vaguely show me the kid's height.

"Probably?" I said.

He looked at the other guy, who merely shrugged. Then he turned back to me.

"Yeah, *probably* this tall. What do I look like, a tape measure?" he said. He had a slight southern accent. "Look, kid, we just want to talk to him."

Even if I hadn't recognized him from a couple of days ago, I'd know that he was likely up to no good. I had no idea who he was looking for, but I definitely wasn't going to help find him, that was for sure.

"Well, mister," I said, "that describes like a hundred kids here. Sorry I can't help more."

That's when it occurred to me that I might be the kid they were looking for. I sort of fit that description, after all, even as vague as it was. Were they looking for the kid who they saw talking to that guy right before they grabbed him? Were they looking for me to get to the package? I swallowed and tried to look like a totally oblivious kid with no worries in the world.

I started past them and I thought for sure that they would stop me, but they just looked at each other again and then stepped aside and let me pass. I wanted to look back to make sure one of them didn't have a gun trained to my head or something, but decided it was safer to just keep walking.

"Hey, kid," one of them said after a few steps.

I turned around to face him.

"You be careful," he said.

A shiver went up my spine. I tried not to let it show. I gave him a nod and kept walking. After maybe twenty feet or so, I heard one of them say something to the other.

"Hey, what about that kid? He's alone, too."

I glanced back. One of them was pointing just past me toward some Dumpsters attached to the school's rear parking lot. They started walking in that direction just as a kid darted out from behind a Dumpster and started running away.

It was Olek.

He looked terrified. The pure panic on his face was enough to tie my stomach in a knot.

The two guys had been walking calmly, but when they saw Olek start to run, they broke into a run as well. Within seconds they were about to rush past me.

I didn't even think about what I did next. Had I had the time to debate the pros and cons of it, I might have decided it was stupid. Or maybe I would have done it anyway. Maybe, just like everything else that had happened lately, I'd have been faced with two options: (1) get involved even deeper into something bigger than I ever could have imagined could exist in this town or (2) ignore it all and go on my way and go right back to my boring, single-track life.

But it didn't matter, because instinct kicked in before I even had a chance to consider all that. The look on Olek's face had been enough to convince me that these two guys weren't chasing him so they could treat him to ice cream and a movie. Let alone the fact that I'd seen these same guys abduct some other guy a few days ago.

So I took off my backpack. Even without Betsy, it was still pretty heavy due to the textbooks inside. Just as the two guys were passing me, I heaved my bag at their knees.

It crashed directly into one of the guys' shins, taking

his feet out right from underneath him. The bag didn't even hit the other guy, but he got pulled down by his partner's desperate flailing. They both crashed onto the pavement pretty hard.

I dived in before they could collect themselves, grabbed my bag, and sprinted toward Olek. He had stopped running when he saw them fall and was just watching us.

"Go!" I shouted.

He stayed frozen for a few more moments but then snapped out of it and started running. I caught him and then motioned for us to head back toward the school.

"This way," I panted.

He nodded and followed me.

I glanced back and saw the two guys getting to their feet. One of them had a trickle of blood running from his forehead down onto his white shirt. They saw us running back toward the school and followed.

"Oh, crap, faster, Olek," I said, through heavy breaths.

"Me? I go slow for you, friend," he said, barely even breathing hard. He started running faster, getting ahead of me by a few feet.

"Go right," I yelled as we approached the school.

He listened and veered right. We ran alongside the

back of the building. I could hear our pursuers' black dress shoes clomping on the pavement behind us. They were gaining pretty quickly.

"Quick, in here," I said, motioning toward the school's back door.

I was pretty sure they wouldn't follow us inside. Even if they were up to no good, chasing down a couple of kids inside of a school was not a good way to remain inconspicuous. I could only hope that the door was still unlocked. It was supposed to have been locked fifteen minutes ago, but our janitor never did things like that on time. It was a pretty safe town. Most people didn't even lock the doors to their own houses every day, so nobody really noticed much if the school doors weren't locked on a strict schedule.

I grabbed the door and pulled. It opened.

"Come on," I said to Olek, and we went inside.

The hallway was deserted. I turned around and saw the two men standing just outside the double glass doors, looking unsure of what to do. They glanced at each other, exchanged a few words, and then the one with the head wound reached out and opened the door.

"They are still coming," Olek said in a panicked voice.

I turned to run and that's when I saw the janitor

standing there behind us.

"What are you kids doing?" he asked. "You have a club or something to get to, or were you just leaving? I need to lock these doors."

I looked back, expecting to see the two men retreating at the sight of the janitor, but they weren't. In fact, they were inside the school now and walking calmly right toward us.

01001011010101000000101010010101010100100100
010101001001001010100101001010101001010100101
1010100001001010010101010010101010101010
000010101010101010011001010101010101010101
010101010101000010100101010010101010
1010100001001010010101010101010101010
0000101010101010011001   10101
001010110101000100100   0100
101010001001010010101   010
                                                101

"**W**OW, MISTER, ARE YOU OKAY?" THE JANITOR ASKED. "You're bleeding, you know?"

The guy reached up and dabbed at his head with a handkerchief.

"Yeah, I was aware," he said.

"You picking up some kids, or . . ." the janitor trailed off, realizing how odd the two men looked.

"No, we're with the school board," the guy said. "We're here for a meeting with Principal Gomez. I just had a little fall outside."

He faked being embarrassed pretty well. Just the same, I couldn't let this farce continue.

"He's lying!" I said. "They're trying to kidnap us!"

The bleeding guy scowled, and the janitor's eyes widened. Then he looked at the two men and back at me, apparently completely unsure of who to believe or what to do. This went above and beyond a normal janitor's duties, I assumed.

"You shouldn't have said that, kid," said one of the guys in suits.

Before the janitor could react, the guy hit him in the side of the head with what could only be described as a wicked roundhouse kick. The janitor flew off his feet and hit the ground. As the guy in the suit raised his hand to hit the janitor again the realization that *I had caused this* suddenly hit me. I was going to be responsible for the janitor getting brain damage, or worse, if I didn't do something.

But they were clearly trained fighters so I would have to hit them hard the first time. I unzipped my bag as I ran toward them, taking out a few pens and textbooks. As soon as I was close enough, I threw one of the books at the guy who had kicked the janitor.

I had been aiming for his groin, but I missed pretty

badly. Fortunately, though, the corner of the book hit him right in the eye and he dropped to his knees and grabbed his face.

Before the other guy had a chance to react, I charged him and drove the pen right into his left thigh. Well, that's what I tried to do, anyway. His leg must have been pure muscle because the pen basically just snapped in half in my hand without even breaking his skin.

But it bought Olek just enough time to react to the situation, because he came charging in and kicked the guy right in the shin.

"Ah!" he yelled, taking a step back.

"That's it," the guy who had gotten a textbook to the eye said. "Enough games."

He scrambled toward me, grabbed my foot, and yanked.

I went sprawling back to the floor, and my vision went black for just a second as my head hit the hard tile. I sat up just in time to see the other guy fling Olek off him with ease. Olek landed pretty hard right next to me.

The two men were on their feet and cracking their knuckles as they moved toward us. I was finding it hard to inhale. So I just closed my eyes and waited to either suffocate or to get beaten unconscious, whichever happened first.

That's when I heard a yell followed by the muffled sound of a kick or punch. I opened my eyes and saw someone attacking the two men in suits with smooth and faster-than-the-eye-can-see kung-fu moves straight out of an action movie. One of the assailants was already on the ground, not moving. The other one was backing away, trying to hold his own against the person who just showed up.

That's when I saw who it was.

It was Mr. Jensen.

But it wasn't Tall Jensen. It was Short Jensen. The scrawny music teacher who was terrified of horror movies and loved show tunes.

Short Jensen made a move toward the one attacker still on his feet. The guy on the ground stirred, but Short Jensen kicked him in the face without even looking, and he was out for good. Short Jensen was like those guys you see in movies who can take down six guys by themselves, except that he wasn't doing crazy jump kicks or wild roundhouses or anything flashy. He was moving fast, and just making little motions here and there, but each one was delivering some kind of devastating blow on the guys in suits.

"Get out of here," Short Jensen said to Olek and me. "Now!"

Even though I was still shocked by what was happening, I didn't need to be told twice. "Let's go," I said, helping Olek to his feet.

We started down the hallway and then I suddenly realized something. If Short Jensen was actually the secret agent, then that meant that I'd delivered Betsy to an unsuspecting and completely clueless sixth-grade teacher earlier that morning. And her countdown was only a few hours away from reaching zero.

I whirled around.

"Mr. Jensen! There's this package that some guy gave to me, it was like a computer or something, with secret data, and it said it was going to self-destruct, and I left it on the other Mr. Jensen's chair this morning!" I knew I was rambling and talking way too fast, but this was obviously urgent.

Short Jensen, who now had one of the guy's arms in a lock that looked like a guaranteed shattered wrist, looked up at me just long enough to say, "It's okay, I'll take care of it. Just get out of here and go directly home, both of you."

We took off running and didn't look back. For some reason, even though those guys had attacked us, I didn't really want to witness what Jensen had in store for them. But there was no doubt that Mr. Jensen had things under control and would not be needing our help.

Once we were at least a few blocks away from the school, Olek and I stopped running and caught our breaths for a few moments.

"Where do you live?" I asked. "I'll walk with you."

Olek nodded, still catching his breath. He pointed up the street and we started walking.

"Thank you," he finally said. "I thought I was . . ."

He didn't finish. Either because he couldn't come up with the right English words or because he couldn't bring himself to actually say it. Not that it mattered either way. Before I could say anything, he spoke again.

"You save my life," he said. "I did not know Agency hire kids."

"Agency?"

Olek grinned at me and nodded.

"Do not worry, Carson, you do not need to pretend. I know you are agent. You save my life!"

I shook my head. "Hey, I would do it again in a second, but I don't know what you're talking about. I'm no secret agent or anything. I'm just some kid who was in the right place at the right time."

As I said this, I couldn't help but to marvel at the whole situation. What kind of crazy secrets did this town have? Here I thought we were just some normal small town in North Dakota where the biggest news stories consist of snowstorms, clearance sales at Walmart, and an occasional fender bender. But apparently the place is teeming with spies, secret agents, evil dudes in suits, unmarked black sedans, talking self-destructing secret message systems, and who knows what else.

And it was awesome.

Olek merely laughed at my denial.

"Yeah, okay," he said, holding his finger to the side of his nose. "I understand, you are not agent."

"Olek, why were those guys after you, anyway?"

He sighed. "Did Agency really not tell you? What do they say, 'Hey, Carson, protect this kid.' 'Why I protect him? Oh, well, this is not important.'" He scoffed. "That sounds like Agency."

"No, they didn't say anything because I'm not . . ." I saw him making that face again. The one that said he knew I was an agent no matter what I said. "Whatever. Sure, I'm an agent."

"I know this." He beamed. "Well, do not worry. My parents, they testify in front of It Do hearing soon."

"It do?" I said.

"Yes, it is I-T-D-O. International Terrorist Defense Organization."

"Terrorist?" I said. "Why would your parents . . ."

"Look, this is where I stay," he said, stopping and motioning toward a normal-looking two-story house. "I must go in now."

"Wait a second." I had so many questions, I didn't even know where to start. But Olek was already halfway up the walkway. "Well . . . I'm just glad you're okay, Olek," I said.

"Ha! Me, also!" he said.

"Okay, I'll see you tomorrow then?" I said.

What in the heck were you supposed to say right after saving someone's life?

"Yes, on bus. We sing again?" he said hopefully as he opened his front door.

"Yeah, maybe," I said with a grin.

0100101101010100000101010010101010010000
01010100100100101010010100010101000101
10101000010010100101010010101010101010
00001010101010100110010101010101010101
01010101010100001010010101010001010101A
10101000010010100101010010101010101010
0000101010101010011001   10101
00101011010100010010   1100
10101000010010100101   010

CHAPTER 19

IT TOOK AWHILE TO DIGEST EVERYTHING THAT HAD HAPPENED TO me that day. And even by the time I went to bed, I still don't think I fully believed that any of it *had* actually happened. I went over the facts in my head:

- Music teacher Mr. Jensen is some sort of secret agent.
- Recent foreign transfer student Olek is wanted by some group of people for some mysterious reason involving his parents and terrorism.

- Data so sensitive that it self-destructs is being exchanged.
- Ominous unmarked sedans and guys in black suits are patrolling the whole town in search of something. Olek? The Package? Both? More?

There were still more questions than answers. And I wasn't sure if I'd ever get those answers.

The next day started off normal enough. By that I mean I rode the bus and made it to school without anyone chasing me or ninja kicking my face or randomly handing me highly sensitive and mysterious information. Olek was on the bus again, though. I don't know what kind of life that kid had lived, but he acted as if nothing at all had happened, as if almost getting kidnapped was just another typical Thursday. The only time he even mentioned it was right before we got off the bus. He tapped me on the shoulder and said, "Thank you again, Carson. Don't worry, your secret is protected with me. Locked in my brain like criminal."

The rest of that morning was pretty uneventful, too. No strange occurrences, no guys in suits, nothing. Even lunch that day was just plain old ordinary chicken and mashed potatoes.

"Ewww," Dillon said as he sat down at our table.

"What are you complaining about now?" Danielle asked.

"Don't you know what they put in these chicken cutlets?" Dillon said. We all groaned because we'd already heard this a hundred times by now, but he continued anyway. "Chemicals, rat poison, industrial sludge, liquefied old tennis shoes. I'm telling you, they're poisoning us little by little, and pretty soon they'll be able to take over the country, because *everyone* eats chicken!"

"Vegetarians don't eat chicken," I said.

Dillon scoffed, "Sure, but do you really think an army of unpoisoned vegetarians and vegans will be able to stop them from taking over? I mean, come on, vegetarians are wimps. They can't build any muscle without protein!"

I didn't even need to ask him who the "they" were in this crazy theory because we'd heard it all before. Dillon was convinced that the NPPC, the National Pork Producers Council, was planning a takeover of the United States, starting by poisoning everyone who ate chicken.

"There's protein in stuff other than meat," Danielle said.

Dillon just laughed. "Oh, Danielle, you're adorable sometimes."

Danielle responded by pouring her milk all over Dillon's lunch tray. She hated it when he was condescending.

"Ah, now I can't even eat my potatoes," Dillon whined.

I looked down at my own potatoes and ran my fork through them. They were pasty, like they were made from some sort of powdered mix rather than real potatoes. I was just about to offer them to Dillon when my fork hit a chunk of something that was most definitely not mashed potatoes, real or powdered.

I pushed at whatever it was with my fork. It looked like a long, thin piece of white paper, like the kind you get in a fortune cookie. Was this some new thing the school was trying? Fortune Mashed Potatoes? It sounded just dumb enough to be an idea Gomez might have actually come up with.

After plucking out the little slip of paper with my fingers, I realized that it wasn't really paper. It was more like a flexible piece of plastic. It's hard to describe, I'd never felt anything like it. It was somewhere right in the middle of paper and plastic.

Then I saw that there was writing on one side, just like

a fortune cookie fortune. I squinted down at the tiny print.

Meet by the track. 10 minutes. Don't be late.

I looked around the cafeteria. How did this get in here? Was it really intended for me? How would it even be possible to make sure that I was the one who got it? I looked toward the lunch line and saw the guy scooping out mashed potatoes. He suddenly looked up, right at me. He stared with a blank face for four or five seconds and then went back to scooping potatoes.

That was pretty much all the sign I needed to know the message was meant for me. The question was, was it legit or some sort of trap? Would I go out to the school track only to find a gang of bullies waiting for me, or even worse, two guys dressed in black suits and black ties?

"Hey, what is that?" Dillon asked.

"Nothing," I said, putting the message in my pocket.

"That didn't look like nothing," Dillon said. "Oh man, did you find something in your chicken? I knew it! See, I told you guys!"

Everyone at the table groaned again.

"Look," I said, standing up, "I gotta go, sorry. I forgot that I had this meeting with a teacher today during lunch."

Dillon, Danielle, and our other friends all looked at

me. This was definitely out of the ordinary. I knew that.

"I haven't been doing very well in math," I said. "I've been too embarrassed to say anything."

This was of course not true, but it was at least semi-believable. I'd always been a mostly C student. Mainly because I spent too much time planning pranks to actually, you know, study and do my homework and that kind of stuff.

"I had to get extra help in science last year," my friend Zack finally said.

"Yeah, and I need extra help in *all* of my subjects," added Ethan.

Everyone laughed at that. Ethan wasn't the smartest guy in the world. But it was okay—he knew it, we all knew it. He was still a good guy. And a great hockey player. He'd make the varsity team as a freshman for sure, maybe even as an eighth grader. He'd actually probably leave the state altogether to go play junior hockey when he turned fifteen and eventually get drafted by the NHL and make millions of dollars and be a part of something much bigger than anything happening around here. Who could feel bad for a guy who was going to travel the country and play a game for a living? He'd be living the dream, after all.

"Thanks, guys," I said, standing up.

They all waved good-bye.

As I walked away, I heard Dillon resume his chicken poisoning rant, followed by the sound of four sets of rolling eyes.

1001101101010100000101010010010101010100100000
1010100100100101010010100101010010100101001010
0101000010010100101010010101010101010101
0001010101010101001100101010101010101010
1010101010100001010010101010100101010100
0101000010010100101010010101010101010101
0001_____00110010101010101010101010
01_____0010101010010101010101001
01_____1010100101010101010101

CHAPTER 20

I T TOOK ME ABOUT FIVE MINUTES TO GET DOWN TO THE TRACK. I wasn't sure when exactly they'd expected me to find the message, so I had no idea if I was late or not. When I got down there, I saw two adults standing next to each other at the starting line.

One of them was Short Jensen. I was guessing that this would be about them trying to explain away what I'd witnessed the past few days. I wondered what kind of ridiculous story they'd try to spin.

"Carson," Short Jensen said as I approached, "right on time."

I smiled and then looked at the other guy. I did a double-take just to make sure my eyes weren't playing tricks on me. The other guy was also Mr. Jensen. The other Mr. Jensen. Tall Jensen.

"What's he doing here?" I asked.

"We work together," Short Jensen said.

"You're a secret agent, too!" I said to Tall Jensen before I could stop myself. "You mean I could have delivered the package to either of you that whole time?"

"Yeah, about that," Tall Jensen said. "What on earth motivated you to open it? You could have hurt someone."

"Sorry," I said, not knowing what else to say.

"Anyway," Short Jensen said, "thank you for meeting us. And getting down here so quickly. I bet you've had . . . a pretty *strange* couple of days, right?"

I nodded. He smiled. He was acting slightly different from the way he did in class. I mean, still friendly but in a more formal sort of way. Professional. Almost cold.

"Well, it's about to get even stranger," he said, the smile quickly disappearing. "Carson, we need your help with something. Something important."

"What kind of help?" I asked.

Short Jensen didn't answer right away. He looked at me for a moment and then took something metal out of his pocket. I almost flinched, but then I saw it was just an old pocket watch, the kind that are round and flip open and closed. He opened it and looked at the face.

"Let me ask you this," he said as he put the watch back into his pocket. "What would you guess is going on right now? Regarding Olek and myself and the package and the other Mr. Jensen?"

I considered my answer carefully. It seemed pretty obvious to me what was going on, but I wanted to think about it first to make sure I got it right. I wanted to prove to them that I wasn't just some dumb kid.

"I'm guessing you're secret agents of some kind," I said. "Working for a government agency like the CIA, but I bet it's not the CIA. I bet it's some agency the public doesn't even know exists. And the package clearly held top secret information, and Olek is someone you're protecting for some reason that deals with national security."

I'd learned a thing or two from Dillon over the years, that was for sure. Of course, I actually knew a little more about Olek's situation than I was letting on, but I didn't want to reveal that. I didn't want to get Olek in trouble for telling me too much yesterday. Plus, they might get suspicious if it seemed like I already knew too much.

The two Jensens exchanged a look.

"There's more to it than that of course, but that's actually pretty close," Short Jensen said. "We *are* protecting Olek. There are certain people who are looking for him, and we're trying to keep him hidden. Olek's safety is directly tied to our national security, as you guessed."

I shook my head. Not in disagreement but in general disbelief that this was actually happening. That Dillon might have actually been right about some of the things he claimed. That any of this could be true, here, now, in North Dakota. There actually had been big and cool and important stuff happening right under my nose the whole time. The question now was, how big was this exactly?

"Is it just you two? I mean, is the whole school full of secret agents?" I asked.

"There are more of us here, yes," Tall Jensen answered. "But it's not the entire faculty. It's only a select handful of us. Most of the school's employees don't know any more about what is going on than you did four days ago."

I nodded. "And you need . . . my help?"

"In a manner of speaking, yes," Short Jensen said.

"Doing what? And why me? I mean . . . I don't know how to be a secret agent. Plus, I'm a kid! How could I possibly be helpful?"

I obviously had no idea how to be a secret agent. But just the same, the idea of working with a couple of real-life secret agents sounded way cooler and bigger than anything I ever could have dreamed of happening in North Dakota. And so I couldn't help but grin as wide as I probably ever had, even before they answered me.

They didn't smile back. To them, this was serious business. So I tried my best to make my grin go away, and I think I mostly succeeded.

"There are a lot of reasons why we need your help," Short Jensen started. "And *if* you agree to do so, then we can tell you more about what those reasons are. What I *can* tell you right now is that you can provide something that our other agents simply can't. I'm not going to lie to you: This could get dangerous. I wouldn't ever ask you to help us if our plans were to send you into harm's way, of course, but as you learned yesterday, sometimes danger and trouble have ways of putting *themselves* in *your* way."

I didn't know what to say to that. So I just blinked.

"Please consider this request carefully," Tall Jensen added. "This job is not something that can be taken lightly. There are lives at stake, Carson. You can help save them."

"What about my family and school? Will I have to leave them behind or something like that?"

"No. Your family will not be made aware of your involvement. As far as anyone will know, you'll still just be Carson Fender, school troublemaker." Short Jensen gave me the slightest smirk before checking his watch again.

"Olek already thinks I'm a secret agent," I said. "Did you know that?"

"We know," Tall Jensen said.

"So what happens if I say no?" I asked, testing them. "Will you guys, like, memory wipe me or something?"

Neither Mr. Jensen even so much as cracked a smile.

"Nothing quite like that," Tall Jensen said. "We'll simply deny any of this ever occurred. You know as well as I do that nobody would ever believe you anyway."

That wasn't technically true. Dillon would believe me. But his point was well made just the same.

"Carson," Short Jensen said. "We don't want you to answer us right now. We really want you to take a night to think it over. This shouldn't be a quick decision. You really should weigh the pros and cons, because once you say yes, you'll be privy to information that you can't unlearn. You'll likely never look at your hometown the same way again. You need to consider all of these things. This meeting will end in twenty-five seconds, at which time you will go back into the school and go on with your day. Please take the night to think this over. Then meet us right here tomorrow morning at eight o'clock sharp and let us know your decision. If you decide not to help us, this conversation never happened. Are we clear?"

Nothing that ever happened to me in my whole life had prepared me for working with secret agents and spies on some sort of covert mission. I mean, a kid in North Dakota has about the calmest, safest life imaginable. How could anyone living here be ready for something like this?

"Mr. Jensen," I said. "How can I really make this decision? I mean, I'm just a kid."

Once again, he didn't hesitate before answering.

"Yes, Carson, you might be just a kid . . . but if you shouldn't be making this decision, then who should?"

With that, both Jensens turned and walked away, across the football field inside the track. The lunch bell rang behind me. I watched them for a few more moments and then headed back toward the school. The whole thing was still too surreal to even take seriously. I mean, it was like the plot of some ridiculous movie on the Disney Channel or something.

CHAPTER 21

THE REST OF THAT DAY PASSED IN A BLUR. I COULDN'T EVEN TELL you half the things I did or said or saw. All I could think about was the Jensens' offer.

On the surface, the decision was still a no-brainer. What kid could possibly say no to getting to work as a real-life secret agent? The choice wasn't even much of a choice at all the way I saw it: I could help them and finally do something extraordinary in North Dakota, finally be a part of something bigger and more exciting, or I could say no and go back to being so bored that I let herds of goats loose on school property just to keep things interesting.

The more I thought about it that night, though, the more uncertain I became. Based on what I'd already seen go down, I knew being a secret agent wasn't like in the movies. It wasn't all fun, cool action scenes where you know everything will be okay in the end. If I did this, I could get killed. I might have to kill. People die doing this. I hadn't even needed to see the Jensens' stony facial expressions to know that. And quite frankly, I wasn't sure if I wanted any part of a responsibility as big as someone else's life. The most stressful decision I'd made up to that point in my life was whether to run my cafeteria prank on pizza day or taco day. It was hard to imagine being responsible for a whole country's safety.

But then . . . it wasn't just another person or a country that needed my help. It was Olek. If I were to choose to do this, it couldn't be *only* because I thought it would be cool to be a secret agent, and that it would finally add something awesome and exciting to living in North Dakota. Olek needed my help.

And it would be my choice. My entire life, I'd been used to everyone making decisions for me. My parents decided where we lived. They bought all my food and all my clothes. I did most of my homework myself, but it was still teachers deciding for me what I was going to study, what I was going to learn. I had even let Gomez decide what I would be doing after school every day, with the whole detention game we played.

The only decisions I had really made for myself, I realized, were the ones about my pranks. That had been my big contribution to the world: messing with people in a humorous fashion. I was finally old enough to start making my own choices, finally smart enough to start figuring things out for myself, and that's what I was spending my time doing? Gluing stuff to teachers' desks?

My whole life I'd always thought I hated responsibility, but maybe that's what had always been missing? Maybe that's why everything in North Dakota had always felt so empty to me? Because nothing I'd ever been a part of made me responsible for anything significant. The only decisions I'd ever made for myself carried no weight of responsibility with them at all. No weight of anything that mattered.

I felt a bit sick to my stomach. There were big things happening in the world. And the people who dealt with them, the people who decided if the world got better or the world got worse, they weren't doing it because someone forced them to. They were doing it because they chose to.

The world, and especially North Dakota, it seemed to me in that moment, was full of people who avoided making big decisions. Now I had a chance to make one myself. What would I do with it?

1001011010101000001010100101010100100000
)101010010010010101010010100100101010010101
L0101000010010100101010010101010101010101
)0001010101010101001100101010101010101010
)1010101010100001010010101010010101010100
L01010000100101001010100101010101010101
)0001   00110010101010101010101
)010   0010101010010101010100
101   1010100101010101010
)0   11010101010101010101

CHAPTER 22

I CRAWLED OUT OF BED AT 7:30 THE FOLLOWING MORNING, WHICH is a really hard thing to do on a Saturday, even if you slept well the night before, which I hadn't. I ate breakfast, got dressed, and told my mom I was heading to Dillon's. But of course that's not where I was headed at all.

I rode my bike to the school's football field, right where I'd met both Mr. Jensens the day before during lunch. I checked my watch as I arrived, I was right on time, just like they'd said to be.

Both Mr. Jensens were there again. Standing in the

exact same spot on the track that they had been yesterday. Short Jensen actually smiled briefly when he saw me pedaling toward them. Tall Jensen gave me a head nod.

"I'm glad you're here," said Short Jensen as I dismounted my bike. "Have you made your decision?"

"I have," I said. "I'm in."

"Good."

"So how does this work? Do I have to go to Agency Headquarters and get some microchip implanted in my leg or something?"

The Jensens glanced at each other.

"No, not exactly," Short Jensen said. "Like I said yesterday, we have a very specific mission for you, one that neither of us would be able to do ourselves. One that only someone like you could do."

"Okay," I said, not sure what he was getting at.

"What he's trying to say is that you're not becoming a full agent," Tall Jensen said. "You're just going to be assisting us with a special assignment."

"Oh," I said, feeling a little stupid.

"But you'll still be doing official Agency business," Short Jensen said. "Let's head inside to my office, where it's secure. We have something we need to show you that will help explain everything."

I locked up my bike at the bike rack near the football field parking lot and then followed them toward the school. Short Jensen turned and spoke to me as we walked.

"We'll first give you a bit of background on what we're doing here. Just the things you need to know in order to complete the mission we've laid out for you. Your involvement is on somewhat of a need-to-know basis within the Agency, so most directives will be carried out through back channels. We'll have you back home by later this afternoon. Do you need to call your parents to let them know you'll be gone past lunch?"

"No, that'll be fine. She thinks I'm at my friend's house."

The Jensens walked a little faster as we neared the school, and it was getting hard to keep up with them. I almost had to jog.

"I've been meaning to ask you something," I said. "Is the janitor in on this? Is he an Agency employee?"

"You're wondering if he's okay, I assume?" Short Jensen said.

"Yeah. That guy hit him in the head pretty hard."

"Yes, he's fine. He'll have a headache for a few days but no permanent damage."

I nodded but noticed he hadn't answered my first question.

"So, let's assume he's not an agent, because I don't think he is," I said. "Then what? I mean, wasn't your cover blown in front of him?"

The two Jensens looked at each other. Then they stopped and turned around to face me just as we reached the edge of the basketball courts adjacent to the school's east entrance.

"It's a valid question, Carson," Short Jensen said. "One that I think deserves an honest answer."

"Okay," I said, suddenly feeling sick to my stomach, sure that they were going to tell me he'd been sent to a holding facility in Siberia for the sake of national security. Tall Jensen spoke first.

"Do you remember yesterday when you asked about us wiping your memory if you declined to work with us?"

"What? Are you serious!?" I said, more loudly than I'd intended. "You really do that kind of thing?"

"Yes, Carson, we have to do that kind of thing from time to time. The janitor will be just fine. It's for his own safety that he not remember what happened. It's much better if he thinks he simply fell off a ladder and hit his head while changing a light bulb in the school that night."

I didn't say anything right away. I just looked down at their feet. They had wiped what happened from his memory. I didn't even know there was a way to do that. It was crazy, and scary. Though, deep down, in a place I didn't really want to listen to, I had to admit it was kind of cool.

"But how? How can you erase only a specific portion of his memory? Do you have some cool sci-fi gadget like in *Men in Black* or something?"

"Not quite," Short Jensen said. "There's a certain chemical we can administer. The right dosage erases certain amounts of a person's short-term memory by increasing the production of GABA, which inhibits neuron activity in the hippocampus, interfering with short-term memory formation."

"You're talking about a drug?" I said.

"Yes, it's a heavily modified form of a drug named Gabapentin. Other side effects are minimal, and if dosed correctly, will not affect long-term memory production or retention."

"You say all that like it's memorized," I said.

Short Jensen smirked. "Yes, Carson, I did memorize that. I'm not a chemist, after all. I only know as much as our team of pharmaceutical scientists tell me. Every cog in the Agency is made up of the most talented and intelligent individuals in their respective fields."

"I hate to interrupt," said Tall Jensen, "but if we stop to answer every question, this might take all day."

"Yes, you're right," Short Jensen said. "No more questions until we're inside."

I nodded.

Then we continued through the empty student parking lot up to the school's east entrance, making our way to Short Jensen's music room office. It was a fairly normal office, I guess, with a desk, computer, two chairs, and small filing cabinet. But it was also different from most teachers' offices in that it had a bunch of old instruments strewn about, including a small piano in the corner.

"Kind of cramped for all three of us, isn't it?" I said.

Short Jensen merely glanced at me and then leaned over the piano keys. He bent down and played a short tune that I didn't recognize. A few seconds later, part of the office wall next to the piano slid away to reveal a narrow metal door.

"That was Agent Hambone's idea," Short Jensen said with a faint smile. "The piano thing. He's our assistant security director. A quirky guy, but good at what he does."

I didn't know what to say to that so I just nodded

dumbly. A secret office within an office? This was getting pretty cool already.

Then I noticed a small digital pad on the front of the metal door. Short Jensen placed his index finger on it and then leaned his face in close. A red line of light passed over his eye and the pad under his finger blinked green.

The door slid open.

"Carson, welcome to my real office," he said as he stepped aside.

0100101101010000010101001010100100000
0101010010010010101010010100101010100101
1010100001001010010101010010101010101010
00001010101010101001100101010101010101
01010101010100001010010101010010101010
1010100001001010010101010010101010101010
00001010101010101001100   0101
00101011010100010010   0100
10101000010010100101   010

SHORT JENSEN'S SECRET AGENT OFFICE WAS BIGGER THAN his teacher office. And it felt a lot bigger because unlike his teacher office, which was cluttered with all kinds of instruments and sheet music and junk, this office was sleek and clean. There was a small metal table with four chairs in the middle of the room and then two larger walls covered with touch-screen glass computer monitors that looked more expensive than my whole house. Most of the computer screens were turned off but a few were on, displaying photographs of people, large blocks of text, and a huge global map with all sorts of symbols displayed on it.

It was basically exactly what I would have expected a secret government agent's office to look like: high-tech and expensive.

"Wow, how can the school not know this is here?" I asked.

"Why would they ever suspect it to be?" Short Jensen asked. "You'd be surprised what sorts of things the truly unsuspecting mind is capable of overlooking."

He had a point. Why in the world would anyone even guess that this was here? I never in a million years would have believed that what I was seeing existed if I wasn't actually seeing it in person at that very moment.

"Have a seat, Carson." Short Jensen motioned toward the metal table in the middle of the office.

Tall Jensen pressed a button on a computer pad just inside the office and the metal door slid shut. Then both Jensens sat down opposite me at the table.

I looked around at all the insanely expensive-looking computer screens covering the walls. There must have been dozens of forty-inch glass monitors.

"The government paid for all of this?" I asked. "I thought our government was almost broke? My social studies teacher said our national debt is like a gazillion dollars."

"The government didn't pay for this," Short Jensen said. "The Agency has a collective of private financiers. To be frank, even I don't entirely know where all of the funding comes from. But I do know that the Agency can't be funded by the government directly. Because then that money has to be accounted for or reconciled in some way. By filtering its funds through private investors, keeping it off the books, the Agency can stay covert."

While Short Jensen answered me, Tall Jensen opened a large black binder sitting on the table. He took out a tan folder stuffed neatly with papers and smaller file folders. He handed me a packet with about twenty pages inside.

"We're just going to start with a brief history of the Agency," he said. "Then we'll talk more about your specific mission. Read this. We'll wait."

I read through the pages. I think it was a brief history of the Agency. The problem was that about 80 percent of the words had a black bar over them so they couldn't be read. I looked up at the Jensens, but they were now shuffling through some other papers and not really paying attention. Were they serious? How could I read a document so redacted that it looked more like a referee's striped shirt than it did a document?

Even the official Agency name on the document was censored, so everywhere it appeared was simply listed as: The ███████████████████ Agency. But anyway, here's what the rest of the document was like:

And it basically went on like that for twenty pages. I finished in two minutes and then looked up again at the two Jensens. When Short Jensen saw I was finished, he reached out, grabbed the folder, and then ran it through a paper shredder built into the middle of the desk.

"Seriously?" I said. "I didn't learn anything from that."

"That's the 'on the record' version," Short Jensen said. "Just so you get an idea of how covert our operations are. But we can certainly have some off-the-record discussions. Just don't ask the name of the Agency. That's classified as high up as Director Isadoris."

"You don't even know the name of the Agency you work for?"

"No," said Tall Jensen, as if it were absurd to think that he would.

"But . . . how do you even know you're working for the good guys?" I asked.

"Let me ask you this," said Short Jensen. "What even makes the good guys the good guys?"

I thought about it. "Because they help people."

"It's actually not that simple, Carson. The actions of historical figures like Genghis Khan were seen as helpful to certain groups of people, but of course when the majority of the people whose life he affected are taken into account, his actions can be classified as easily more harmful than good. But then it gets even more complicated when you start to consider how his actions affected the world's development. What I'm getting at is that it's a more complicated question than you think. So many of the choices we make don't break down to 'good' and 'bad.' There are choices I've made as an agent that I know were right, but I still regret. You yourself chose to come help us today, but I bet you had at least some misgivings. Was your choice 'good' or 'bad'? Or is it rather hard to tell?"

I nodded. He made a good point, even if it did give me a headache to think about.

"Okay, let's get down to business, guys, shall we?" Tall Jensen said.

"Yes, we do have a lot to cover," Short Jensen said. "Here is what you need to know about the Agency, unofficially. The Agency was founded in the late 1950s, originally coinciding with the installment of the Air Defense Command Base north of town. Shortly after that base opened, they established a Semi-Autonomous Ground Environment sector, which was basically a giant blast-resistant concrete building housing three 250-ton computers. These SAGE computers processed air surveillance information and sent the data to the Air Defense Command units. With me so far?"

"Uh, sort of," I said.

I'd lived my whole life just twenty miles south of the Air Force base he was referring to, but I never had learned its history or knew what any of this military technical jargon meant. He continued without clarifying anything.

"The SAGE unit was essentially a computerized watchdog, commissioned with keeping our country safe from aerial attacks from the north. The Agency was established covertly in conjunction with that program. It started with just two operatives whose sole job was to detect espionage in and around the residential populace in the vicinity of the Air Defense Command Base and the SAGE unit, and the eventual nuclear missile silos that the Department of Defense planned to install in the area."

I had known about the nuclear missile silos. Everyone who grew up around here had seen or at least heard about the missile silos before. There were supposedly close to two hundred nuclear missile silos built underneath farm fields all across the state of North Dakota. I'd driven by some of them on the way to the lake before. They weren't much to look at, really. They were marked simply by a patch of concrete with a small building on it surrounded by a chain-link fence. Plus two guys in military fatigues holding M-16 machine guns stationed outside.

"So the Agency was originally just here to make sure no Russian spies found their way to North Dakota since there were going to be nuclear missiles and bases built here?"

"Yes," Short Jensen said. "We were originally a counterespionage unit. However, in the years that followed, as the base and the Agency grew, the prime directives also changed and expanded. It was around the early 1970s that the major focus began to include counterterrorism along with espionage prevention, as well as some more unusual functions. Our goals and directives now shift weekly. The threats to our country, foreign and domestic, are constantly evolving. An organization as large and public as the CIA cannot keep up with this. That's where we come in.

"We now have several branches across the country with an ever-evolving roster of agents and support personnel, each with their own purpose and mission and hierarchy chain of command. But every action ultimately goes back to only a handful of individuals, most prominently Agency Director Isadoris. These days our duties include much more than simply counterterrorism and espionage prevention. Some of the folks here in the Dakota office like to call us the Chaos Breakers."

"Chaos Breakers?" I said.

"People just want things to be normal, particularly where they live. Their desire for such is so strong that they sometimes overlook the presence of odd things, strange people, weird events, et cetera. You feed off this desire with your pranks, Carson. You like to see what happens to people when the abnormal happens, when chaos erupts."

I nodded. He was right. I pulled my pranks as a way to break up the routine. To make things more exciting. To cause chaos. But it wasn't quite the same. I didn't want there to be fainting goats running around town permanently or anything. Even I understood that wouldn't really work, as funny as it would be.

"But I'm just having fun," I said.

"Right, but there are others who are not. There are certain groups of people looking to cause chaos for a variety of reasons. Sometimes for money, sometimes for political purposes, sometimes simply out of principle or ideology. That's where the Agency comes in. We are the people here, behind the scenes, making sure that chaos doesn't happen. That people in this country are able to go on leading their normal lives. We're the ones who make the tough decisions so that the rest of the people out there don't have to."

I wondered just how many things Dillon had been right about all these years after all. I mean, Dillon was basically the opposite of the people Short Jensen was talking about. He saw the odd, the suspect, the dangerous everywhere, even in the most normal things. There were so many of his theories that could be tied to possible Agency activity. His claims that he'd found wiretapping devices all over the school, stories of seeing strange men following him, even the cameras in the swallow nests he had seen yesterday. The list went on and on.

"So, what are you doing here?" I asked. "I mean, there can't be *that* many threats to the country here in North Dakota. Shouldn't you be off in some other country doing spy stuff?"

"Both Mr. Jensen and myself are officially considered Field Operative Operational Coordinators, meaning we generally oversee the planning and execution of a wide variety of missions taking place all around the country, and sometimes even off American soil. This is something technology allows us to do from here, without needing to travel as often as agents did in the past," Short Jensen said. "Or as much as Active Field Operatives need to."

"So you're kind of like the bosses or supervisors to other agents?" I said.

"Yes," Short Jensen said.

"And I'm never allowed to tell my parents and friends any of this stuff?"

"Well, a part of us asking you for help is trusting you with this information," Short Jensen said. "We can't stop you from telling them, of course. In the end, the decision is yours—you must weigh the benefits of telling them against the risks, to them and to you."

Would they even believe me anyway? Would I want them to? Who knows what kind of danger I could bring on them if I did tell them?

"All right," I said. "So what's next, Mr. Jensen? Or, Mr. Jensens, or, whatever, you know what I mean."

"I think it's time you started calling us by our agent names, Carson," Short Jensen said with a smile. "I'm Agent Nineteen."

I followed his look over to Tall Jensen.

"Blue," Tall Jensen said. "Agent Blue."

"Cool," I said. "Do I get a codename, too?"

Agents Nineteen and Blue exchanged a quick look.

"Of course," Agent Nineteen said. "You will be known by the codename Zero."

"Agent Zero," I said to myself.

Agents Nineteen and Blue nodded at me. It was a pretty cool codename. I mean, the fact that I had a codename at all was awesome; it didn't even matter what it was. *I have a codename*, I thought to myself again. It barely even sounded real in my own head.

There was definitely no turning back now.

1001011101010100000101010100101010100100000
1010100100100100101010010100010101010010101
010100001001010010101010010101010101010101
000101010101010100110010101010101010101010
1010101010100000101001010100010101010100
010100001001010010101010010101010101010101
0001   001100101010101010101010
010   0010101010010101010101001
01   1010100101010101010101
            11101011101101010101010
CHAPTER 24

"**N**OW, WITH YOUR AGENCY DEBRIEFING OVER, WE'RE GOING to finally discuss your primary directive," Agent Blue said.

"Remember how I said before that there are groups out there looking to cause chaos?" Agent Nineteen said.

I nodded.

"Well, right now we're particularly concerned with a group referred to in Agency circles as the Pancake Haus."

"The Pancake Haus?" I said, wondering if I was supposed to be laughing at this part.

"Yes, it's a goofy codename, I know. It's a long story."

I nodded. "Pancake Haus, got it."

"At this point, the Pancake Haus don't appear to have any political affiliations or unified causes. The few things that have been attributed to them, either allegedly or confirmed, haven't seemed to have had much of a purpose, unfortunately, other than to simply wreak havoc in some way."

"Okay, so what does this have to do with Olek? Is this Pancake Haus you're talking about after him? Why?"

"Well, as you may have guessed, Olek is not his real name," Agent Nineteen said. "But that's the name by which we're referring to him and shall continue to do so. Olek's parents are in witness protection. The Agency has been tasked with providing protective custody for his parents and, in turn, Olek as well. Olek's family ran a small fabrication business in their home country, where his dad unwittingly helped to create housings for bombs that were used in recent terrorist attacks in several countries, including a recent failed attack in Great Britain. He did not know what he was creating. He thought he was fabricating a housing system for a pesticide trailer for a commercial farming operation. With me so far?"

I nodded and tried not to look as frightened as I

was getting. Bombs? Terrorists? This was definitely no game. I couldn't believe they were actually telling me this much. But I supposed if I was going to help them, I had to know why.

"When Olek's parents found out what his father had been doing, they contacted the US government immediately and were referred to us. With Olek's parents' help, we were able to track down and apprehend several prominent terrorists thought to be behind the attacks. They are now awaiting a trial hearing in front of the International Terrorist Defense Organization."

"International Terrorist Defense Organization?" Olek had mentioned that the day before. "Why are the terrorists even getting a trial? Can't you just lock them up forever?"

"That's a great question," Agent Blue said. "It's not quite like you see in the movies where America just captures terrorists and locks them up without a proper trial. The ITDO was established to independently try those accused of international acts of terrorism. Olek's parents' testimony is critical to our case. If they're not able to testify at the trial in five days, then these guys will likely walk free. Free to cause more harm to innocent people."

"And so," I said, starting to put the pieces together,

"terrorists are after Olek to use him as leverage? To keep his parents quiet?"

"Precisely," Agent Nineteen said.

"Not just Olek, either," Agent Blue added. "They're also after his parents. There have already been two attempts on their lives. All three of them have been split up and are being kept in three different locations for extra security. It was difficult to convince Olek's parents to let him go, but after the first attempt on their lives, they were convinced that Olek would be safer somewhere else."

"Why is the Pancake Haus involved?" I asked. "Are the terrorists part of that group?"

"As far as we know, the Pancake Haus has no affiliation with these three terrorist leaders. They've most likely been employed by a third party to kidnap Olek and then auction him off to the terrorist groups who are affiliated with the accused individuals. Or maybe the Pancake Haus wants them set free simply to cause more chaos."

"So why move Olek here, to North Dakota of all places?" I asked.

"Integrating him into a school's population in a small town is the best way to hide him while also allowing us to watch over him. Also, North Dakota is the last place anyone would ever look for someone."

"Except," I said, "they *are* looking for him here."

"It appears that way," Agent Nineteen said.

"So if they already know he's here, then what can I possibly do to help?" I asked.

"That's what we wanted to show you," Agent Nineteen said and then nodded at Blue.

Agent Blue walked over to a small locker in the corner of the office. He scanned his fingerprint on the door. The locker clicked open. Agent Blue took something out, closed the locker, and then set the object in the middle of the table.

"Betsy!" I said. I had kind of hoped to never have to see her again.

"Who?" Agent Nineteen said.

"Oh, uh, yeah, that's what I started to call this thing," I said.

"Did it remind you of Betsy Hummel or something?" Agent Blue asked as he opened the lid and exposed the screen.

"Actually, yeah," I said, surprised that he would know how annoying Betsy Hummel was. But I guess maybe teachers noticed more than we all thought they did.

"Well, this thing is actually a PEDD," Agent Blue said. "Agent Orange's PEDD, to be precise."

"Pet? Huh?" I said.

"No, his *PEDD*," Agent Nineteen said. "It stands for Personal Encrypted Data Device. All field agents are issued a PEDD for transporting encrypted data too sensitive to be exchanged via wireless modes of communication."

"Like I said, this was Agent Orange's PEDD," Agent Blue continued. "We'd lost all contact with him in recent weeks. He was supposed to be stationed in Omaha, Nebraska, running surveillance on a smuggling outfit. What can you tell us about how you acquired this?"

I told them all about what had happened. About the sweaty guy in the suit. What he told me. That I saw him get forced into a dark sedan by a few guys with pasty faces and guns. I even told them about seeing the black sedan driving in front of my house a bunch of times.

"Well, that all fits what we've found," Agent Nineteen said to Blue.

"And our suspicions that Agent Orange has likely been compromised," Agent Blue agreed with a slow nod.

He turned to face me again.

"Do you think you'd be able to recognize the guy who gave you the package if we showed you a photo lineup?"

"I don't know, maybe," I said.

Agent Blue then took a piece of paper from his

briefcase. He put it on the table in front of me. There were eight color headshots printed on the paper. I looked at each of the faces. They all looked so similar, it was hard to say. Plus, I had been so distracted that day I hadn't really gotten all that great of a look at the guy.

I shook my head.

"I'm sorry, I can't really say for sure. It might be this guy, but they all look so similar. . . ."

I pointed at one of the pictures.

They exchanged another look and then nodded at each other. "Agent Orange," said Agent Blue, and he tilted Betsy's screen so that all three of us could see it.

"Well, we've partially recovered the PEDD's contents," he said as he started pressing some buttons on Betsy's monitor. "The data was secured using some older Agency encryptions, which is why it's taking longer than usual to decode the entire hard drive. But here's what we've found so far: Apparently Agent Orange had intercepted a coded message from Pancake Haus' chiefs to their field agents. He must have immediately abandoned his station in Omaha and rushed here to deliver us the message. We're guessing his interception wasn't totally clean, which is why he left his post without following the proper channels, and also why he had enemy agents on his tail. Here is the message he lifted from the Pancake Haus communiqué."

I looked at the message now displayed on Betsy's screen:

```
To Field Operative Cells A3554 and CV76:
Code level 7A.
The Agency is harboring Playground in
Minnow, North Dakota. School Unknown.
Your assignment is to conduct sweeping
surveillance of the three middle schools
located within Minnow city limits.
Playground identity is unverified but
stands approximately 4' 10" and has
dark hair. Subject will be new in school
and will not have many acquaintances.
Concentrate on individuals eating lunch
alone, at recess alone, walking to and
from school alone. Detain and question all
individuals matching this description.
```

"Playground?" I said.

"We surmise that's their codename for Olek," Agent Blue said.

"So they know Olek is here, but just don't know what he looks like?" I asked.

"Correct," Agent Blue said.

"And as you read, they're looking for someone who fits Olek's description. New to town, mostly alone, doesn't seem to quite fit in," Agent Nineteen added. "We've been able to further validate this information via interrogation of the two individuals who pursued you and Olek Thursday after school."

"That actually makes sense," I said. "Those two guys were just asking me questions. And they didn't actually chase after Olek until he started running away."

Agent Nineteen nodded. "We believe Olek tipped them off. Only people who have a reason to run would run in that situation."

"But how did they find out Olek is here?" I asked.

"We're not sure," Agent Nineteen said. "We're hoping either the rest of the information encrypted in Agent Orange's PEDD or further interrogations of our detainees will answer that for us. Although we have reason to suspect that they may have coerced the information from another field agent of ours who went missing several weeks ago."

Coercion, interrogations, compromised agents. This

whole thing was suddenly starting to feel very, very real to me.

"So now that they know he's here, why not just ship Olek off to some other town? Why not keep hiding him somewhere else?" I asked.

"At this time, it wouldn't be wise to pull him from school enrollment," Agent Blue said.

"Why not?"

"For one, we have a stronger presence here than anywhere else. This is our turf, he's still safer here than anywhere else. And second, there are only five days left before Olek's parents testify. Planning and initiating transport to a new location will take several days, and moving him will likely bring even more attention his way, especially if the Pancake Haus has agents on the ground here. We think it's better to hide him in plain sight. Which is where you come in."

I nodded. Then I paused.

"Wait, what?" I said.

"As you saw in that encrypted message," Agent Nineteen explained, "Pancake Haus is looking for a kid on his own, a kid with no friends. A new kid. Someone who is alone when he arrives to school, when he goes home, when he eats lunch. That's likely why they singled out both you and Olek that day. You guys were alone when they attempted to question you. They won't be looking for a kid with friends, a kid who looks comfortable at school, like he's been here for a while. So that's what we need you to do: make Olek *belong*."

Nineteen was right. Helping Olek fit in with other kids at school was something no adult would be able to do. At that moment, the idea of a kid helping out real-life secret agents suddenly seemed less ridiculous than it ever had before.

"So that's your primary directive. Befriend Olek. Get him in with your friends as well. Sit with him at lunch, bring him with you when you hang out with other friends outside of school. But also keep an eye on him, and watch out for enemy agents or suspicious activity."

I nodded, thinking that this actually might not be too hard. I mean, I already liked Olek and apparently he liked and trusted me, too. That was a pretty good start as far as I was concerned.

"A few other details," Agent Blue said. "Starting today, for any Agency matters, you will be known simply by your codename, Zero. This codename is not to be spoken or even thought about in the presence of non-Agency personnel. Is that clear?"

"Yes, sir," I said, nodding.

"Good. If we need to contact you further, we'll send you messages via Agent Chum Bucket, who currently doubles as one of your school cafeteria food service providers. Messages will be delivered *only* in this format, or in person via Agent Nineteen or myself. Any other message you may receive via any other means shall be disregarded and reported to either myself or Agent Nineteen immediately."

"What if I need to contact you guys after school hours?" I asked. "Like if Olek and I are in danger or something?"

"You will have this," he reached into his briefcase and took out what looked like a very small keyless entry remote for a car.

It was about an inch wide, two inches long, and almost cardboard thin. It had only two buttons, a green one and a red one, and no other markings of any kind.

"What is that?" I asked.

"Should you ever find yourself in a situation where you need backup, press and hold down the red button for ten full seconds," Agent Blue said. "If you have a message or need to communicate with the Agency in a non-emergency situation, press and hold the green button for ten full seconds. In either scenario, someone from the Agency will contact you within the appropriate amount of time."

"But how will they know where I am?" I asked, not understanding how pressing a red button on a tiny remote could possibly help me in an emergency situation.

"There is a GPS tracking device inside the remote," Agent Blue said. "All of this said, we don't anticipate you needing to use it. If you integrate Olek effectively, they'll have no reason to suspect either of you. Besides, we're going to have Agency eyes on you both at all times up until the trial. We'll have your back if things go south."

"There will be further instructions awaiting you when you get home," Agent Nineteen added. "That covers everything for now. Any questions?"

Of course I had hundreds. But at that moment, I didn't think I could handle any more information. I had my mission, and so I just swallowed and shook my head.

0100101101010100000101010010101010010000
010101001001001010100101001010100101
101010000100101001010100101010101010
000010101010101001100101010101010101
010101010101000010100101010010101010
101010000100101001010100101010101010
000010101010101001100 10101
00101011010100010010 100
10101000010010100101 10

CHAPTER 25

GOT BACK HOME AROUND NOON.

Everything felt different. Like the kitchen. The kitchen used to feel like the heart and soul of the house. But now it just felt like a plain old kitchen. It seemed emptier to me. I didn't like the feeling at all.

I saw my brother watching TV in the living room. I said hi to him and then headed downstairs to my bedroom. Almost as soon as I opened my computer, I got an incoming Skype call from Dillon. That was another thing about Dillon—he pretty much only communicated via written notes, in person, or with Skype.

It wasn't that he thought video chat was better or cooler than phone calls or text messages or anything. He just simply refused to use phones of any kind. He said all communications via telephone, including texts, were monitored and recorded by some massive database, and that your communication histories were used for all sorts of manipulative reasons. Or something.

Dillon didn't really like Skype much either, but we had to communicate somehow. It's not like we could send smoke signals to each other across town. Anyway, being friends with Dillon entailed accepting a lot of crazy stuff. Or at least I used to think it was all crazy. Given what had happened to me in the last forty-eight hours, Dillon's theories didn't seem all that outlandish anymore.

I clicked on the Answer button on my computer screen. Dillon's face filled my monitor. He was wearing his tin foil gloves again. (Don't ask.)

"Hey, Carson, what's up? Where have you been all morning? I was convinced that the Candy People had gotten to you or something."

I just stared at him. I tried to say something but didn't. Or couldn't. Why wasn't I answering him? Likely because I had spent the morning inside a secret office belonging to a covert government secret agent instead of hanging out with Dillon and Danielle like usual.

"What's wrong?" he asked. "What are you up to?"

"Oh, nothing. It was just an interesting day," I said.

"Why, what happened?"

I was being an idiot. That was the last thing you ever wanted to say to Dillon, even under normal circumstances. My first ten minutes of having an official secret agent mission and I was already close to blowing my cover. Maybe deep down I even wanted to blow my cover. At least on some level.

"Just a lot of weird stuff happened," I finally answered him. "But it was all family stuff, so nothing you'd probably care about."

"Oh," he said, looking disappointed. "Well, do you want to go to the circus with Danielle and me later tonight? There's also that new milk bar right next to the circus grounds that we still need to check out."

"Milk bar?"

"Yeah, I guess it's like a regular bar, but instead of serving beer, they serve, like, custom flavored milk. So kids can go, too."

"That sounds pretty cool," I admitted.

"Yeah, so you want to go today with us then?"

I had totally forgotten about the circus. Under normal circumstances, I would have gone for sure. Now, I just didn't think I could deal with it. Not only that, but the circus felt even more boring and ordinary to me now than ever before. Even with the addition of a new custom milk bar or whatever.

"I wish I could, but I can't. I have to help my mom with something," I said. "Maybe next weekend?"

"Okay, yeah, whatever," he said. "What about tomorrow? Do you have any time to hang out at all this weekend?"

"Maybe. I'll let you know. But if not, then I'll see you Monday at school, okay?"

He nodded. I had to admit I felt pretty bad.

"Okay, well, I'll see you," he said and disconnected the call.

I was just about to stand up when I noticed the small, tan envelope sitting on my desk. It was sealed and had two words written on it in black marker:

Open Me

I remembered Agent Nineteen saying there would be further instructions waiting for me at home. So I opened it without hesitating. Inside the envelope was a flash drive with two more words scrawled on it in tiny print:

Play Me

I plugged the flash drive into my computer. It contained just a single WAV file. My heart raced as I double-clicked it. One hour into my mission helping out a top secret agency and I was already receiving top secret messages. This was probably the fastest my heart had ever beat in my life. Heck, it was probably the fastest anyone's heart had ever raced in this whole state.

The media player opened. I saw right away that the video was just over two minutes long. I clicked play and the screen went black. Then white text appeared on the screen:

Agency transmission R436T00 will begin in 15 seconds. Please ensure the security of this information by turning down the volume on your device and positioning yourself in a secure location.

There was no one in my room but me, obviously, but I still instinctively looked around. I turned down the volume on my computer to the second to lowest setting. Then I quickly stood up and closed my bedroom door. I sat down at my desk again and waited, trying to keep from going into excitement-induced cardiac arrest.

Agent Nineteen appeared on the screen in front of a black background.

"Zero, thank you again for agreeing to help us. Your main objective is to incorporate Olek into the social fabric of your school as deeply and seamlessly as possible. It is imperative that it appears as if he's been here for years. Accomplishing this can be done by adhering to the following three directives:

"Directive One: You must ask your mother if Olek can stay the night at your house for the next five nights, until his parents are able to testify at the trial. Make up any reason that is not the truth to get them to agree. Olek will be coming over tomorrow, so get her permission before then. Your house will have undetectable Agency protection and surveillance for the duration of his stay to ensure the safety of your family. It is important that Olek is seen with other kids as often as possible. There is no greater way to achieve this than to literally have him by your side at all times outside of school classes.

"Directive Two: Incorporate Olek into your group of friends at lunch. Not only should he become your friend, but he should become theirs as well. The more friends Olek has, the better.

"Directive Three: Be on the lookout for any suspicious activity. Report anything unusual to either myself or Agent Blue.

"We know you can do this, Zero. If you execute your mission properly, Pancake Haus will never suspect Olek as their target. Right now they're looking for a needle in a haystack. We need you turn to Olek from a needle into just another piece of hay.

"This message will self-destruct in ten seconds. I highly recommend you discard the flash drive immediately. End transmission."

With that, the screen went completely dark. Wow, my first Agency transmission. I still couldn't believe . . . wait, did he say self-destruct in ten seconds?! What was it with these guys and self-destructing messages?

I imagined my whole computer exploding, and then without thinking about it further, I ripped the flash drive from the USB port and threw it into the trash can next to my desk. Then I dived behind the foot of my bed and covered my head, waiting for the *BANG*.

When a few seconds passed and nothing happened I peeked around the side of my bed. The flash drive was still sitting inside the wire-mesh trash can. Maybe the detonator was defective? Or maybe it was some sort of a secret agent practical joke?

But then I smelled it. The smell of burning plastic. I walked over and looked inside the trash can. A thin tendril of white smoke drifted up from the flash drive, and the burning smell got stronger. After a few seconds the smoke started dissipating, as did the smell. Then it just looked like an ordinary flash drive again, sitting inside the garbage can.

0100101101010000010101001010100100000
0101010010010010101001010010101010100101
1010100001001010010101010010101010101010
0000101010101010011001010101010101010
01010101010100001010010101010010101010100
1010100001001010010101001010101010101010
0000101010101010011001   101010
0010101101010001001   1001
10101000010010100101   010

CHAPTER 26

LATER THAT NIGHT, AFTER DINNER, I HELPED MY MOM WITH dishes and made my pitch for Olek to stay the night with us until the following Monday.

"Why so long? And on school nights?" she asked.

"Because he's got nowhere else to go!" I said. "Their house got infested with termites . . . *and* rats. Great giant ones with tails so big they crack like whips when they run, and, and . . ."

"Carson, I got the point already!" My mom had always been grossed out by rats.

"Okay, well, anyway," I continued, "apparently his parents' insurance will only pay for a single hotel room. Which means he'd have to share a bed with his younger brother and sister. And his younger brother Juri has some weird gastrointestinal problem that causes him to fart like every ten seconds, and not just normal farts, either. Juri's farts are like . . ."

"Enough with the farts," she said, making a face again.

I had a feeling the grosser the story, the more tired she'd get of listening to it. And the more tired she got of listening to it, the sooner she'd cave in."

"And so I thought maybe he could stay with us until their house gets fixed next week."

She sighed as she stirred the soup she was making for dinner. "I suppose that'd be fine."

The next day, I anxiously awaited Olek's arrival all afternoon. My dad was out of town, as usual, my mom was at a movie, and my brother was off doing who knew what with his pals. So I sat alone on the chair next to the front window in the living room and waited. My hands were almost shaking I was so anxious for Olek to get here. I still wasn't sure how they were planning to sneak him in without being seen.

But they didn't sneak him in at all. In fact, sometime

late in the afternoon, Olek came pedaling up the street on his bike with a backpack slung over his shoulders. Which was surprising at first, but then made sense the more I thought about it. It all fit in with the "hiding in plain sight" plan. Pancake Haus still didn't know who Olek was, so he needed to do all the things normal kids did, like ride their bikes to their friends' houses and not be escorted there by secret agents in government-issued SUVs.

I told him to park his bike in the garage and then welcomed him inside.

"I expected them to, like, drop you off with armed security or something," I said. "I can't believe they let you ride over here alone."

"I was not alone. They follow me whole time, just in case," Olek said.

I looked out the window and down the street both ways. I didn't see anybody else. Except my neighbor, Moe, who was out mowing his lawn again. That weirdo must mow his lawn at least three times a day. I never did get that. Didn't adults have enough stuff to worry about as it was? Why add extra stress by freaking out over how their grass is growing?

"I don't see anybody," I said.

"Exactly the purpose they want," Olek said. "I ride my bike over here. They watch just in case. Easy as cake."

"It's easy as pie," I corrected him.

"Yes, this what I say, piece of pie."

"No, that's . . . never mind."

"Where is room? I would like to embark in sleep now."

"You want to take a nap?" I asked. I didn't think anybody between the ages of seven and forty took naps.

"Yes," he said. "I am awake since three a.m."

"Since three?! That's crazy early," I said.

"Is okay, as they say, early bird get many intestine worms in guts."

I laughed. "Close enough. What were you doing up that early? Agency stuff?"

"Oh, no," he said like that was a ridiculous notion. "I was playing this game you have. . . . Furious Ostrich."

"Angry Birds?"

"Yes! Is great game! Very much addicting."

I grinned and shook my head. "Come on, I'll show you my room."

He followed me downstairs and I put his bag on my bed.

"This your bed?" he asked.

"Yeah, but it's yours now. At least for as long as you're

here. I'm going to sleep here on the floor." I pointed at a sleeping bag rolled up in the corner.

"Thank you," he said. "Is very nice thing you do."

"Look, you can nap now, I guess, but later we should play some Xbox. Do you know how to play Xbox?"

"Yes, of course! Does polar bear not vomit inside forest areas?"

"No, the saying goes . . . ah, never mind. Anyway, I'll see you when you get up later, okay?"

"Yes, is good," he said, plopping down onto the bed.

I went back upstairs to the living room and sat on the big loveseat. I must not have realized how exhausted I was, likely due to everything that had happened to me the past few days, because before I knew it I was suddenly being awoken by the sound of laughter. I opened my eyes to find myself slumped over on the couch in our living room. I was disoriented at first and had no idea where I was. I *never* take naps. I couldn't believe I'd actually fallen asleep.

Once I'd finally woken up enough to realize where I was, I looked up and saw Olek in the kitchen helping my mom make dinner. He was sitting at the table peeling potatoes. My mom was laughing almost uncontrollably at something.

"What's going on?" I asked, rubbing the crust from eyes.

"Carson, you didn't tell me your friend was so funny!" she said through her laughter.

"I didn't want to spoil the surprise," I said, glad they were getting along.

"Dude, your friend is hilarious," my brother said from the chair across from me. I saw the Sunday Night Football game on TV.

"You're a hit!" I said to Olek.

"Like Beatles song?" he asked.

"Sure," I said, again wondering where he came up with this stuff. "Like a Beatles song."

He grinned at me and kept working on the potatoes.

"Mom, isn't it kind of racist to make the Russian kid peel the potatoes?" I said.

"Carson!" she said.

Olek laughed. He laughed harder than I'd ever seen him laugh before. This only made my mom, brother, and me start laughing as well.

"This not so bad," he said, finally. "In some country, potatoes are peeled with dirty fingernail."

As my mom heard this, she had to stop chopping because it was unsafe to laugh that hard with a knife in your hand.

After a loud, fun, and very funny dinner, Olek and I excused ourselves. Well, that was after Olek offered to help with the dishes. I'd nudged him with my elbow when he offered. He was making me look bad.

But my mom refused to let him help anyway.

"You're our guest," she'd said. "Don't be ridiculous."

And so we headed downstairs to my bedroom to relax and try to have some fun. It might be cool for Olek to have one full night with a friend that wasn't filled with abduction attempts or hiding out in whatever safe house they had him at before he came to stay here.

We played video games for a while. He was better than I'd expected. I'm not sure why I thought he might be terrible, but it either had something to do with my obviously ignorant assumption that they didn't have Xbox in his home country or else just that being endlessly pursued by a rogue terrorist cell distracted him from practicing his video-game technique.

He said he loved hockey and so that's what we played for most of the night. But after a while, we switched it off and just talked and joked around until we fell asleep.

The next morning was my first day at school with an official secret agent mission to accomplish. Once Olek and I were on the bus, I felt like I couldn't talk to anybody. So for the first little bit I sat there and looked out the window. I had no idea what I was looking for, but I figured it didn't hurt to be looking just the same.

But whatever it was I was looking for, I didn't see it. Or maybe I did and just didn't know it. Either way, I soon realized that I was being ridiculous. My directive was to be friends with Olek, to try and make him look like a normal kid. Which I was doing a pretty miserable job at so far.

"Hey, Carson," Olek said, breaking my long and unintentional silence. "We sing today?"

"No, I don't think so. Not today."

"Yes, is strange thing, anyway," he said. "Singing on bus. Who does this?"

I laughed. I had no idea if he intended to be so hilarious or not, but it didn't really matter either way. It was no surprise my family loved him so much. And it wasn't just because his broken English was funny, which I was starting to think was intentional anyway. He was just so *genuine*. He said what was on his mind, and asked questions he wanted answers to. It never felt like he was pretending to act a certain way to fit in like pretty much every other kid did at least a little.

It almost felt like he was immune to the boring North

Dakota single-track mindset in some way. He simply did and said what he felt, without worrying about how odd it may be. That's just not how most people in North Dakota acted. And I loved that about him.

We rode in silence for a while. I kept looking out the window, watching for any sign of those ominous unmarked sedans. Then I realized I was doing it again, ignoring my directive, and instead just being paranoid.

"So what kind of stuff were you into back home?" I asked.

Olek thought about it for a second and then said, "Well, I like eating strawberry jam with spoon, hypnotizing elderly turtles, collecting old horse hooves to build fort with, um, oh yes, I also really like standing in middle of park pretending to be tree that suffers from serious tree disease, Comandra blister rust."

I stared at him with my mouth hanging open. I wasn't sure what to say so I didn't say anything. But then I caught a glimpse of a small smile twitch at the corner of his mouth. He was messing with me!

"That was good, Olek, you really had me," I said.

He grinned. "Yes, your face was like that of corpse. I joke of course. Except for part with strawberry jam. I do love eat strawberry jam with spoon. In USA, why is eating jam with spoon not okay to do? People say this is gross to do, but is no different than eating gummy bear! It make no sense."

"I have no idea," I said through a laugh.

But I had to admit, he made a good point. Why did people think it'd be weird to eat jelly with a spoon? It's just fruit and sugar, the exact same stuff that's in fruit snacks.

"No, but for real," he said, "I like mostly same things kids here do. Like play video games, watch movie, play hockey and football. Not your game of throw oblong thingy and then give each other brain damage. I mean, *futbol*. Or, soccer is what you call it here. . . ."

"Was it hard to leave all that behind? I mean, your country, your friends and family, everything?"

His smile faded, but only for a few seconds and then it returned and he shrugged.

"Yes. But is okay, because I make new friends, yeah?"

"Yeah, definitely," I said.

He kept smiling and then nodded at me.

"Is good," he said.

0100101101010100000101010010101010010000
010101001001001010100101001010100101
10101000010010100101010100101010101010
000010101010101010011001010101010101010
0101010101010000101001010100101010101
10101000010010100101010010101010101010
000010101010101010011001   10101
001010110101000100101   0100
1010100001001010010101   010

CHAPTER 27

THE ONLY CLASS OLEK AND I HAD TOGETHER WAS FOURTH period. Which was perfect, because then we could walk to lunch together. I wanted to sort of warn him about Dillon before we got there.

"So, I have this one friend who is kind of . . . weird," I said. "He might say some strange things."

"Ha, is no problem. All Americans say strange things."

"Yeah, well, okay, but this one might say some really crazy things. He might even accuse you of being a communist or something."

"Me, a communist?" Olek said with a grin as if that was the funniest thought a person could ever have. "Why he think this?"

"Because of your accent, likely. But don't pay attention to any of that. He just watches too many old action movies."

"Okay, no need worry."

"Good. You're a positive guy, Olek," I said.

"I know. I have to be. Is essential," he said.

I knew what he meant. He had to be because being torn away from your country and family and stuck someplace you don't want to be (hey, nobody wants to go to North Dakota) sucks, despite what he said earlier. He would always brush things off as no big deal. If he didn't, the crappiness of his situation would probably just drown him. That's another thing I loved about him—he *never* complained. About anything. I mean, everybody complains. All the time. And it was always annoying to listen to unless you were the person doing the complaining. But Olek never did. He always saw the bright side of everything. I never knew how cool it could be to hang out with a person like that, because I'd never before met a person like that.

By the time we got to the cafeteria and went through

the lunch line, everybody was already at our usual table. There was one chair open, the one I usually sat in.

"Hey, guys, this is my new friend, Olek. He's going to sit with us today," I said.

A few of them nodded, but before anyone else could say anything, Dillon said, "Well, there aren't enough chairs. The table's full, see?"

I figured Dillon would be a jerk to Olek, but I didn't expect it to start up the moment we got there. Dillon has always been a little tough until he gets to know you. Mostly because he's always skeptical of people. He thinks everyone is hiding something.

I walked over to the next table, grabbed one of the five empty chairs and slid it over next to mine.

"Now there are enough," I said.

Olek and I sat down.

"A little crowded now," Dillon whined, but everyone ignored him.

I shot Olek an apologetic glance, but he looked completely unfazed. He smiled and waved at everybody. I introduced them all, and Olek said "hi" aloud after every single name. It was hilarious. Danielle was barely keeping it together.

"So why are you here?" Zack asked.

"To eat lunch, of course. I am so hungry, I will eat like cow," Olek said.

Everyone laughed at this, and Olek smiled.

"You're supposed to say *eat a cow*," Danielle corrected him.

"Ah, yes, but why I want to eat whole cow?" Olek asked.

We all laughed again.

"No, I meant, like, why are you in America?" Zack asked. "Are you a foreign exchange student?"

"Is long story," Olek said. "I move here with my mom to live with my aunt's third cousin. My dad contract insane goat disease back home. Very contagious. Was safer for me to move here for school year."

They kept peppering him with questions, which he gamely answered. Everyone seemed to be finding it pretty amusing, including Olek. Then Dillon tapped me on the shoulder.

"Where were you all day yesterday?" he asked. "I thought we were going to hang out. You never answered any of my Skypes."

He had that suspicious gleam in his eyes that I used to find more funny back when I didn't actually have anything to hide.

"Family emergency," I said.

"What, did someone die?"

"Actually, yeah," I said, hoping that would encourage him to drop it.

"Oh, oh, sorry," he mumbled. I'd clearly succeeded. But now I felt bad.

"It's no big deal; it was my grandma's cousin. I only met her like twice when I was really young. Plus she was like ninety-nine years old."

He nodded. He took a few bites of spaghetti and then finally asked what I knew he'd been dying to since we sat down.

"So what's with the commie?"

"He's not a communist, Dillon," I said, rolling my eyes.

"Fine, whatever, you know what I meant. Besides, it's not like you could possibly know that. He could easily be a commie."

"He's just a kid, Dillon. How could a kid have a fully formed political ideology? Besides, he's really funny and nice. Plus, he never complains about anything. Can't I make new friends?"

"Of course you can," Dillon said. "It's just that . . . well, something weird is going on in this town. And it all kind of goes back to when he first showed up."

I looked at Dillon. He was as serious as ever. And it dawned on me that this was likely not the first time Dillon had been right about something. That he might have been right about a lot of things. There *was* something weird happening in this town. And now I was right in the middle of it.

"You mean weirder than all the other stuff you claim is happening?" I said, trying to pretend like I didn't know he was right. "Like weirder than how you think the town newspaper is really a front for an illegal exotic pet store?"

"They are! Read the classifieds. It's all code for what they have in stock!"

I laughed and shook my head. "Look, just try giving Olek a chance. He's really cool."

Dillon sighed and then nodded. "Okay, I will. But he better not try to turn any of us, or I swear . . ."

"Dillon, he's not a communist," I said. But this time, I'd said it a little too loudly.

Everyone at the table looked at me. Then slowly their heads turned toward Olek. He paused for a few seconds and then started laughing. Everyone else joined in, even Dillon.

Relieved, I finally got a chance to start eating my spaghetti. After my first bite, I noticed something digging into my gums. I reached up and spit it out as casually as I could when I was sure nobody was looking at me. It was another tiny piece of paper.

> Meet me by the south cafeteria exit at exactly 12:37.

CHAPTER 28

NEAR THE END OF LUNCH, AT EXACTLY 12:37, I EXCUSED MYSELF and emptied my tray into the garbage. Then I left through the south cafeteria exit. I saw Agent Chum Bucket immediately, by the doors to the kitchen itself. He was a huge dude, the sort of guy you'd never expect to be a school lunch lady. Or lunch guy. Cafeteria worker. Whatever. He was pretty tall, had arms as thick as most people's legs, and his forearms were covered in tattoos. But he'd worked in the cafeteria as long as I'd gone to school there and he was by far everyone's favorite lunch worker. He'd always give us extra helpings of whatever he was serving if we asked, even though he wasn't supposed to.

He motioned toward a door across the hall with a nod of his head. Then he looked around and unlocked it and led me inside.

Agent Chum Bucket flipped on the light and I saw that we were in a small pantry of sorts. It was a narrow, deep room with a small walkway surrounded on both sides by towering shelves filled with canned and boxed foods of all kinds. There was one shelf that contained at least seven drums of fruit cocktail as big as my mom's car.

"Zero," he said. "Welcome to my lair."

I wasn't sure if I was supposed to laugh or not, because his face remained totally serious. So I just nodded.

"Agents Nineteen and Blue asked me to give you a few things that may come in handy at some point, in case you're ever in a pinch." He grabbed a small duffel bag sitting in between a massive box of individually wrapped saltine crackers and a ninety-gallon jar of pickles.

"Cool!" I said, unable to help myself. I mean, I was getting some secret agent gadgets. How could I not be pretty excited about that?

"Yeah," Agent Chum Bucket said with a grin as he

opened the bag. "It is pretty cool. Okay, first up is this."

He held up an ordinary-looking pen.

"What does that do? Is it like a bomb, or a memory wiper?" I asked.

"No, it's going to be your best friend in personal defense in a desperate situation," he said. He clicked the pen so that the ink part was exposed.

It looked just like an ordinary pen at first glance. But then he beckoned me to look closer. At the tip there was the tiniest, thinnest needlepoint, only about a centimeter long.

"Click again to release the toxin," he said. "Your would-be attacker will be incapacitated in less than three seconds."

"It kills someone in less than three seconds?" I didn't really even like the idea of having that kind of power in a simple pen.

"No, this particular pen merely contains a tranquilizer. A very powerful one, though, so don't experiment with it on any kids, right?"

I nodded.

He next showed me what looked like a patch of skin from someone's palm. I thought it was gross, which made him laugh. Anyway, you stick that on your own palm and inside was a small pocket containing a simple lock-pick needle for handcuffs. There was also another one for my other hand that contained a small razor for other types of restraints, like tape or rope.

Agent Chum Bucket spent the next few minutes showing me how to pick handcuff locks. At first it was sort of difficult, but once I got the hang of it, I realized that handcuff locks were surprisingly easy to pick.

"The bad news," he said, "is that more and more people, including law enforcement, are no longer using standard handcuffs. So you may find the razor palm more useful. Then again, if you ever get captured, you likely won't live long enough to use either of them."

I swallowed and nodded. He merely shrugged.

"This next one is pretty dangerous, so be careful with it," he said, holding up a fruit roll-up.

"Seriously?"

"Yes," he said solemnly.

"What would I do with that, give somebody diabetes?"

"That, or you could use it to incinerate their guts," he said.

"Eww," I said.

Agent Chum Bucket laughed. Then he explained how

inside the wrapper was not an ordinary fruit roll-up. This fruit roll-up was really a plastic explosive that could be remote detonated with a tiny transponder also inside the package. He showed me how it worked by unrolling one of them. It smelled and looked and felt like a real fruit roll-up. But then he stuck it to a giant plastic jug of mayo. Inside the fruit roll-up wrapper, tucked in the corner, was a small square of paper, barely the size of my pinky fingernail.

"That's the detonator?" I asked.

He grinned and nodded. "Watch closely."

He held the paper on the tip of one finger. Then he delicately peeled one layer of it off like a sticker. Inside the peeled paper square was the smallest-looking computer chip I think I'd ever seen. He held it really close up to my face so I could see a small red light illuminate.

"Peeling the paper arms it," he said. "Now press down and . . ."

He pressed his thumb over the chip as he said this, and suddenly there was a very muted bang just as a small spray of mayo splattered against a box next to the jug. The explosive had only left a small hole about the size of a golf ball in the jug of mayo.

"Cool," I said.

"It's not all that powerful by design. It's intended to be used for doors that have electronic locks or other such situations. Not to be used to try and demolish a car or anything." He threw the package away. "Anyway, this next one is my personal favorite," he said, reaching back toward the table.

It was a small tube with skin-colored straps. He attached it to the underside of his wrist. Then he grabbed what looked like a miniature clip of bullets and clicked it into the tube.

"You ever see in cartoons where there are smoke bombs that some wacky character throws to the ground and then vanishes in a poof of smoke?"

I nodded.

"This takes that a step further, in a way," he said. Then he pointed his wrist across the small storage room, and a second later I heard a faint clicking noise.

Smoke literally exploded out of whatever it was he'd just launched across the room. Only it wasn't smoke exactly; it was more like thick fog. It had a slightly chemical odor, not like the charred smell of real smoke at all. But just the same, I couldn't believe how much it was able to generate so quickly. In less than five seconds, the small storage room was completely filled with a thick fog. I could barely breathe.

Agent Chum Bucket must have flipped a switch to a ceiling fan or something, because there was a whirring noise coming from above me, and a short time later the fog began to clear.

"It has a range of fifty yards, and is completely harmless to inhale. It will linger for close to thirty minutes in confined areas but less than two in open air," Agent Chum Bucket said.

"Cool," I said, thinking of how handy this would be for pulling off pranks.

Next he showed me a small pair of contact lenses that would apparently allow me to see in the dark, and also a small grappling hook disguised as a set of keys.

"How does it work?" I asked, holding the keys.

"Here," he said, taking them from me.

The key ring looked pretty normal. It was just one ring with two normal-looking keys, one larger car key, and a small flashlight keychain. He flipped a switch on the bottom of the flashlight keychain, then he grabbed the car key and pointed it at the ceiling. He pressed down and held the key fob part of the car key for several seconds.

The metal key part exploded up and embedded into

the ceiling. There was a thin wire attached to the end leading back down to the key ring. He gripped the keys tightly and then pressed a button on the small flashlight, and suddenly the wire was retracting and pulling him up toward the ceiling.

He let go and dropped back to the ground after a few feet.

"How did that hold you up there?" I asked.

"The wire is three-hundred-pound strength. The key pad itself is equipped with a state-of-the-art anchor system, capable of suspending weight for several hours from most surfaces. It will latch on to almost anything, so just point and aim."

He showed me which buttons did what and how to use it. How to unlatch it, everything.

"It's so simple my three-year-old could use it," he said at the end of the demonstration.

"Wow, thanks!" I said.

"No problem. Odds are, you won't need to use any of these, but it's best to have them just in case." He helped me load all the gadgets into my backpack. "All right, you'd better get going. Your next class starts pretty soon, right?"

1001011010100000101010010101010010000
1010100100100101010010100101010010
010100001001010010101010010101010101
0001010101010101001100101010101010101
0101010101000010100101010010101010100
010100001001010010101010010101010101
0001
010
01
011001010101010101010
001010101001010101001
1010100101010101010101
10101010101010101010

CHAPTER 29

LATER THAT DAY, WHEN I WAS WALKING THROUGH THE HALLWAY to my seventh-period algebra class, I felt a hand grab my shoulder. I turned around, expecting it to be one of my friends.

But it was Mr. Jensen. Or, I mean, Agent Nineteen.

"Hi, Carson, I've got that information you requested about the musical tryouts," he said, holding out a folded piece of paper.

"Uh, thanks," I said as I took it.

"Hope to see you there," he said and then walked away.

I stopped walking and leaned against the wall right there in the hallway, unfolding the paper and looking at the handwritten words.

Olek is at his most vulnerable after school while you're in detention. It would be better if you're with him that whole time. You need to find a way to get Olek into detention with you for the whole week by the end of seventh period.

Ingest this note.

I folded the paper back up into a square. Was he serious? Seventh period started in like ninety seconds. How was I supposed to get Olek detention while I was in a whole different class?

I ran after Agent Nineteen.

"Mr. Jensen, wait!"

He stopped and turned around and I could tell by his expression that he was annoyed I'd chased after him.

"How am I supposed to carry this out? I have class now!" I said.

"Figure it out," he said almost coldly. Then he whispered, "And don't ever break your cover in the hallway. You shouldn't need my help; getting detention is what you're supposed to be good at, right?"

Then he turned and walked away again. This time I knew better than to follow him. Besides, he was right; this was supposed to be my thing. It should be a piece of pie, right? I mean, getting detention was my specialty.

I looked back down at the note again, rereading the last line.

Ingest this note.

Did they seriously want me to eat it? I shrugged and stuffed it into my mouth and chewed. It tasted dry and stale, like you'd expect. I mashed it up in my mouth until it was nothing but a slimy ball of goo and then swallowed it.

I basically spent the first few minutes of my seventh-period class practically banging my head on the desk trying to think of what to do. I had just fifty minutes of class left to figure out how to get to Olek and then get him in trouble.

Getting out of my class wouldn't be that hard. My algebra teacher, Mr. Kittson, was pretty reasonable. If I told him I had a stomachache, he'd definitely let me leave to use the bathroom. The problem was getting into Olek's classroom.

Olek had Mrs. Larimore for seventh-period English,

the same teacher I had for homeroom. The same lady who was already mean and strict as it was, but who I'd also peed my pants in front of last week. If I just showed up at her classroom unexpectedly during seventh hour she'd not only refuse to let me inside for a second, but she'd also probably give me three more weeks' detention.

But the good news was that I could also use her to my advantage. It meant that Olek wouldn't have to do much to get detention. It was just a matter of contacting him somehow. Like I said before, she once gave some kid two weeks' detention just for bringing his pet gerbil to class, and that was . . . Wait.

The whole plan hit me so suddenly that I almost fell out of my desk.

"Having problems?" Danielle asked next to me.

"No, I'm actually perfectly fine, thanks," I said back. "But, I gotta go. I have some shenanigans to pursue."

She grinned. "What are you up to this time?"

"I'm sure you'll hear about it," I said as I grabbed my backpack and stood up.

I went up to the teacher's desk and told him I had a terrible stomachache. He wrote me a hall pass and I left. I headed immediately toward Ms. Colby's classroom. As

I walked, I was formulating what I would need to say to her in order to acquire what I needed for my plan. But it turned out that luck was on my side: Her classroom was dark and empty. Seventh period must have been one of her off-hours.

But that created another small problem: The classroom door was locked. It didn't take long for me to realize that I had just what I needed to get around that in my backpack. I took out one of the three fruit roll-ups that Agent Chum Bucket had given to me.

After unwrapping it, I stuffed the soft cherry-flavored roll-up into the door, right next to the lock. Then I took a few steps back and pressed the small detonator like he'd shown me. There was a soft *boom*, followed by smoke drifting away from the door.

I grabbed the handle and pulled. The entire doorknob came off in my hand, and I heard the inside knob clatter to the floor on the other side. I gaped at the metal doorknob in my hand and then at the hole it had left behind in the door.

Oops.

I shrugged and then pushed the door open. It closed behind me, and I gently set the loose doorknob next to the other one inside the classroom. I felt sort of bad but figured that doorknobs couldn't be too expensive to replace. Right?

Either way, I needed to stay focused. I only had thirty minutes left. I had to hurry in order to make sure Olek got detention by the end of the period. I grabbed the two supplies I'd come here for and snuck back out into the hallway. Next stop: Mrs. Larimore's class.

I walked by her room as casually as I could and saw that she was up front giving a lesson of some kind. The thought crossed my mind that I could just run in there and try to get Olek in trouble somehow, but Mrs. Larimore would send me down to Gomez's office before I'd be able to implicate Olek. There was no choice but to carry out my plan.

I went to the end of the hallway and turned the corner, taking a deep breath. This was the part of the plan that I was most worried about. I had no idea if it would work. But I had to try.

The hallway was closed off at one end by a set of double doors that led to the gym. The other end was slightly longer and led to one of the school's exits. There were a few classroom doors along the way, but they were all closed.

I dug inside my bag for the key ring grappling hook

and looked up at the metal vent cover on the wall, just below the ceiling. I honestly had no idea whether that vent would lead me to Mrs. Larimore's classroom. It's not like I had a blueprint of the school schematics memorized or something. But I figured it had to. Wasn't that the whole point of air ducts? To connect all the rooms in one building to the same air conditioning and heating systems?

After looking both ways down the short hallway I was in, I aimed the keys at the ceiling right next to the air vent cover. I pressed the button like Chum Bucket had shown me, and the keys fired up and lodged into the ceiling.

After attaching the keys to my belt, I grabbed the stuff I'd gotten from Ms. Colby's room and then pressed the retract button. I slowly started upward. I couldn't believe that the thin cord and a motorized lift that small were able to hoist me to the ceiling with such ease. It was pretty awesome.

I dug a penny from my pocket and unscrewed the screws holding the vent cover in place. It fell open on its hinges. After hoisting the item I'd gotten from Ms. Colby's room up into the vent and pushing it forward and out of the way, I did the same with my backpack. Then I reached up and grabbed the inside of the vent. I released the grappling hook so I was now dangling from the vent by just my grip. I pulled myself up and into the air duct. It was a pretty tight squeeze but after enough wriggling and squirming, I was inside the small, metal rectangular tube. The object from Ms. Colby's room and my backpack were in front of me.

I had no choice but to leave the vent hanging behind me. There was no way I'd be able to turn around and close it in this tight space. So, I just started crawling forward in the vent in the direction of Mrs. Larimore's classroom.

It was surprisingly easy to find. After passing over one other classroom, I could see kids through a vent below me and I heard Mrs. Larimore's voice talking about dangling participles or some nonsense.

From this particular vent opening, I could only see about ten kids, none of who were Olek. I looked up ahead in the duct and saw a second vent just ten feet ahead. I crawled forward, pushing my supplies ahead of me.

I lifted them both over the next vent opening and then peered down through the slits. It appeared that luck was finally on my side. I was almost directly above Olek. Not exactly, but definitely close enough to execute my plan.

There were only fifteen minutes left of class, so I had

to hurry. I found the backsides of the screws holding the vent cover in place. They were just loose enough for me to unscrew with my fingers. Once they were mostly unscrewed, I leaned down close enough to the vent to see the front of the classroom.

Mrs. Larimore was still up front talking. Every few seconds, she'd turn around and point to something she'd written on the whiteboard behind her. While I waited for the right moment, I began prepping the delivery.

I took out the roll of twine I'd taken from Ms. Colby's classroom and then opened the lid of the hamster cage. The hamster cage I'd also taken from Ms. Colby's classroom. I took out a hamster. It trembled and squeaked. I felt sort of bad for it, but it's not like it would get hurt. In fact, if anything, it might end up enjoying the brief freedom.

The hamster thankfully stayed still while I tied one end of the twine around its midsection. I was careful to get it tight enough to hold it but not tight enough to suffocate it or something. I did the same thing to the other three hamsters. Then, all I could do was wait for the right moment.

I watched the class go on for what seemed like hours but was really only like six minutes. Then, just like that, it was suddenly time to act. Mrs. Larimore had just finished her lecture and turned around to erase all the junk she'd scribbled on the whiteboard.

Right as she started erasing, I pushed the vent open. Then I grabbed the four hamsters in both of my hands and held them out over the opening. I let the four strands of twine slowly slide through my palms.

The hamsters began their descent.

When they were about halfway down, dangling in a big furry bunch, someone must have seen them because I heard a soft gasp below me. Thankfully, Mrs. Larimore was also mostly deaf. So she just kept on erasing the board in big, slow arcs.

I continued lowering the hamsters. They were now right in between Olek's desk and the kid next to him. The kid next to him saw the hamsters and looked up at me. We locked eyes and I put a finger over my lips. He grinned and then nodded at me.

Another perk to being the school prankster: Kids almost always went along without question. I started swinging the hamsters back and forth, to get them closer to Olek. By this point I could now hear a lot of suppressed giggles and murmurs below me. Most of the class had now seen the hamsters dangling from the ceiling. Mrs.

Larimore just kept on erasing, but she was nearly finished.

As the hamsters swung back and forth like a pendulum, I let out more string. Then, as they arched over Olek's desk, I let go. They landed on his desk with a soft plop. One of them slid all the way across his desk and right over the edge. But the kid next to Olek, who had been watching the hamsters swing back and forth the entire time, reached out and caught it before it hit the ground.

Right after I let go of the strings, I grabbed the vent lid and quickly closed it. Then I leaned over and watched the fun develop below me.

For starters, as soon as the hamsters landed on Olek's desk, he shouted out in surprise.

"Ah! It rain giant rat!"

The class erupted into a chorus of screams and laughter. Mrs. Larimore turned around instantly. She didn't react for the first few seconds as she tried to piece together what exactly was happening.

Then she saw the hamsters on Olek's desk. They scrambled around, looking for somewhere to go. The strings of twine attached to them were on Olek's shoulders and one piece was in his hair.

"Olek!" she shrieked. "What is the meaning of this?!"

Olek grabbed the loose strings and stood up, holding the hamsters out in front of him. They dangled together and began squeaking in unison. Some kids laughed, some squealed in disgust or delight, or maybe a little of both.

"They rain from ceiling like dog and cat!" Olek said. "What is happening?"

He started walking toward Mrs. Larimore with the hamsters dangling in front of him. She gasped and took a step back.

"Get them away from me!" she shouted.

"They come from sky!" Olek said. "Is giant rat rain!"

"You're in big trouble, young man," Mrs. Larimore said. "Principal's office, right now!"

I took that as my cue to get the heck out of there. I still needed to find my way to a safe spot to get out of the school's ventilation system and then back to class before the bell rang. But I knew Mrs. Larimore would never believe Olek. He was as good as busted. I felt bad for him, as he must be incredibly confused, but I was sure that once I explained why I had to frame him, he'd understand.

01001011101010100000101010100101010010010001
01010100100100100101010010100010101010010101
10101000010010100101010100101010101010101
00001010101010101001100101010101010101010
01010101010100001010010101010010101010100
01010000100101001010101001010101010101
000010   0011001010101010101010
001   0010101010010101010100
01   1010100101010101010101
       CHAPTER 30   1010100101010101010101
                    1101010101010101010

"**O**LEK, DID YOU GET DETENTION?" I ASKED, WHEN I CAUGHT up with him after school.

"Yes!" he said. "You not believe what happen in my class! It rain fat rats from ceiling!"

I laughed. "I know. I was there."

"What? How is this possible?"

I explained to him what had happened and why I'd done it.

"Ah, yes, is good work," he said when I was done. "Is very smart plan."

"Good, I'm glad you're not mad at me."

I spent most of detention looking out the window. Right after detention is when those enemy agents had been snooping around on Friday. I assumed that's when they might try again. About halfway through the hour, I saw a black unmarked sedan roll slowly by the school.

I glanced at Olek. He had apparently been watching, too, because he looked at me with wide eyes. I wanted desperately to write him a note to discuss an exit strategy, but the detention supervisor, Mr. Walsh, was about as no-nonsense as teachers could get. He had a sixth sense for note passing. No matter how sly you were, he always knew somehow.

So we both just sat there and stared out the window for the rest of detention. We never saw the car again, but we did see something else suspicious. There was a handful of men in matching uniforms walking around the school grounds. They looked like phone company technicians, because the logo on their uniforms formed the letters MCMC, which I was pretty sure was our town's phone company: Minnow Communications Management Company. But when I looked closer, I wasn't so sure the uniforms were authentic. For one, they were spotless, as if they'd never been used for actual work. And two,

I never saw them once do anything that could be considered phone-related. They were basically just snooping around.

Olek and I exchanged another look.

When detention ended, we met by the door outside where the late buses picked up. My bus wasn't there yet, as evidenced by the group of kids waiting. But between us and the bus stop were a few of those suspicious, fake telephone company guys talking to one another.

"We should be safe out there with that pack of kids waiting for the bus," I said.

Olek nodded. I dug the tranquilizer pen that Agent Chum Bucket had given me out of my bag. Just in case.

"Okay, let's go together. Don't look at any of those guys standing around on the lawn. Remember, they won't suspect two kids who look like longtime friends with nothing to hide," I said.

"Right," he said. "Is very cape and knife."

I almost laughed in spite of the fact that I felt like I was going to have a heart attack or something. I was pretty sure he'd meant cloak and dagger.

"Okay, so as we pass, laugh like I just told you some joke," I said.

He nodded.

We opened the door and started walking out. We got no more than eight steps when two of the fake phone service technicians came out of nowhere and walked right by us. As they passed, Olek laughed and then I did, too, my grip on the pen tightening.

"And then he actually did it!" I said, pretending I was telling some hilarious story. "He actually puked on his parents, in their bed, while they were sleeping! On purpose!"

Olek laughed again, but this time it sounded even more genuine. The two guys walked by without even looking at us. We joined the group of kids waiting for the late buses.

"It works?" Olek whispered.

"Yeah, I think so," I whispered back. "But don't turn around to check. It might look suspicious."

All in all, I felt like it had been a pretty good first day. I guess there was always the possibility that those guys really had been phone-company employees and not enemy operatives at all, but I was going to consider it a victory regardless.

Once we got home, I plopped down onto my bed, and Olek sat on the floor. We played video games for several hours, until my mom called for us to come up and help her with dinner. After we'd eaten, Olek and I went back to my room again to hang out. I opened my computer to check my email, and as soon as I did, I got a Skype call from Dillon.

"Want to come over?" he asked.

"No, I'm pretty tired," I said. "I evaded capture from two secret enemy agents today."

"Yeah, whatever," he said.

Olek, who was across the room and out of view from my computer's camera, smirked at me.

"Really, though, I just have a lot of homework," I said.

"I'm telling you, doing your homework is only helping them."

"Helping who?" I humored him.

"The secret league of animal rights activists who are planning a takeover of our school," he said. "You know, since there's a top secret animal testing facility built miles underneath the school building and all. Anyway, they're wearing us down with the assignments, so we'll be weak when they finally make their move! I already told you this."

"Yeah, but Dillon, I have to do enough of my homework to at least get Cs or my parents will ground me."

"Fine, suit yourself. Being grounded is better than

becoming a slave to a bunch of animal rights radicals. But whatever."

I laughed, and so did Olek.

"Who's that? Is someone over there?" Dillon asked.

"Yeah, Olek is staying with me for a little bit, remember?" I said. I had told him and Danielle about Olek's "infestation problem."

"Oh, yeah, well you guys can both come over?" he suggested hopefully.

Then Danielle's face popped into the screen.

"Come on, Carson, we want to go check out that new milk bar over by the circus. I heard they have bubblegum-flavored milk!"

I thought that sort of sounded gross, but perhaps I was going about this the wrong way. I think I was saying no because being out in public and trying to hide a protected witness was exhausting. Just telling one little lie is easy, but lying constantly to your friends with no room to make even one mistake was a lot harder than it had seemed.

But the thing was, my primary directive was to make Olek fit in. To act like a couple of normal kids as much as possible. And hiding out in my house all the time like a couple of bearded hermits who are building a castle out of dry skin flakes or something was *not* helping Olek appear like a normal kid. The right thing to do, whether or not it was the easy thing to do, was to go.

It was my mission directive after all.

"What do you think, Olek? Want to get some milk?"

"Yes, please, thank you," he said.

"Yeah, okay, we'll be over in a little bit," I said to Dillon and Danielle.

They smiled.

"All right, see you soon!" Danielle said.

I closed the computer. Olek was grinning ear to ear.

"What?" I asked.

"I never have American milk-bar beverage before," Olek said. "I cannot wait for this to begin."

"Well, then, let's get going."

0100101101010100000101010010101010010000
0101010010010010101010010100101010100101
1010100001001010010101010010101010101010
0000101010101010100110010101010101010101
0101010101010000101001010100101010101010
1010100001001010010101001010010101010101
0000101010101010100110010101010101010101
0010101101010001001010101010101010100101
1010100001001010010101010010101010101010

CHAPTER 31

MEDLOCK'S CUSTOM MILK BAR WAS A REASONABLY SHORT bike ride from Dillon and Danielle's house. It was already dark outside by the time we got there. I hated that about fall and winter in North Dakota. I didn't know what it was like in other parts of the country, but here it got dark fairly early starting in the fall, and by winter it would be completely dark by 4:30 p.m. each afternoon. Even after spending my whole life here, it still bothered me.

But this new milk-bar place was brightly lit and packed with families and kids. It was huge, with several rows of red booths, and nearly all of them were filled. It had opened right before the school year started and had been pretty popular. Apparently it was modeled to be like an old-fashioned ice cream place, except that instead of ice cream their specialty was custom-made milk. Although apparently they served old-fashioned ice cream made from their milk as well. I didn't know what made old-fashioned ice cream old-fashioned. To me ice cream was ice cream, and I'd never had ice cream I didn't like.

We got in line, which practically stretched out the door. But that made sense—it was prime dessert time. As we waited, I noticed that most of the employees were teenagers. Except for one guy who was like thirty, who I guessed was the manager or owner.

"So, are you guys going to get ice cream or are you gonna try the custom milk?" I asked.

"I'm going to try the milk. I've heard it's amazing," Danielle said.

"Just ice cream for me," Dillon said.

"I'll probably get both actually!" Danielle said.

"I never have ice cream before," Olek said.

"What!" Danielle said. "How could you live this long without ever having ice cream? This is going to change your life forever, Olek."

"You've really *never* had ice cream?" Dillon asked. "Is ice cream illegal in your country or something?"

I threw an elbow at Dillon and he yelped. But it didn't matter. Olek just laughed it off. I think he sort of understood Dillon by now and just took it as a joke.

"No, I have ice cream, just not American ice cream. In my country, ice cream is not always dessert food. In my country, number one ice cream flavor is boiled goose skin."

"Eeewwww," Danielle said.

"Seriously?" Dillon asked.

Olek nodded. "Yes, but this is not my favorite flavor. My favorite flavor is kidney bean."

We all laughed, even though I was pretty sure Olek had not been joking.

We were just a few people away from ordering now.

"What kind do you want?" I asked Olek. "I'll get yours."

"That's so sweet of you!" Danielle said.

I just grinned and tried my best not to let my face get too hot. The truth was my mom had given me some money before we'd left, so it's not like I was personally buying it for him. But still.

"But keep in mind, they don't have boiled duck or

kidney bean flavor," Dillon said, I think genuinely trying to be helpful.

"I like chocolate," Olek said.

"Sounds good," I said.

Then we were up.

"What can I get you kids?" the older guy working the counter asked.

I ordered chocolate ice cream for me and Olek.

"You're not going to try our custom milks?" he asked. "I mean, our ice cream is good, but our custom milk is really our specialty. I designed them myself, you know."

I noticed that his nametag said *Mule Medlock*. I remembered the name of the place was Medlock's Custom Milk Bar.

"You're the owner?" I asked.

"Yes, sir. Custom milks! The idea just came to me one night in a dream. Think about it: Everything is custom-made these days to suit everyone's unique tastes. Why not milk? Any kind of milk, any flavor, we can make it. We've got all different kinds. One percent, two percent. I could have some one-and-a-half percent mixed. We also have many flavors—mint, mango, tarragon. Want peppermint seven-and-a-half percent? We can do that. Or popcorn-flavored twenty percent? We got you covered there, as well. Literally, whatever the customer wants."

"Uh, okay, what do you recommend?"

"I know just the thing," Mule said.

He turned around and dug inside of the cooler and took out two glass milk bottles. He poured us each a small sample size of milk. One was pale purple, the other pale orange.

"Okay," he said, "try these. Here, a mango five percent, and this one is a grape seven-and-a-half percent."

He slid the little cups across the counter.

I picked up my cup of milk and took a drink. It was thick, way thicker than the skim milk my parents normally bought. But it was also amazing. I expected it to just be like a milkshake or smoothie, but it was something else entirely. It was smooth, creamy, cold, and had the perfect amount of grape flavor.

"Wow," I said, genuinely meaning it.

"Right?" he said with a smile.

Olek took a drink of his and then promptly downed the rest of it.

"Oh, this is like drinking cash money!" he said, practically shouting. "May I try more please, Mr. Mule?"

"Of course!" Mule said, delighted, "I'm so glad you like them! Here, try the peanut-butter-banana three percent.

And, please, call me Medlock."

He poured Olek a cup of thick yellowish milk. Olek took a drink and then finished it again quickly with a slurp.

"This taste way better than boiled goose skin ice cream!" he said.

Medlock just beamed, clearly proud of his work. Dillon and Danielle laughed at Olek's reaction. Medlock poured them each a sample as well. They took a drink and joined our ranting and raving about how good it was.

"Carson, you must try peanut banana!" Olek exclaimed.

I'd never seen him so excited. Mule Medlock poured me a sample before I could even reply. I took a drink. It was even better than the grape milk.

"I want to change my order," I announced. "Forget the ice cream. I'll have a medium peanut-butter-banana milk."

"Yes, me, too," Olek said.

Dillon and Danielle also ordered milks instead of ice cream.

"Sure thing!" Mule said and then got our orders ready. He put them all on the counter. "Here, on the house. Just be sure to tell all your friends and family."

"Wow, thanks!" I said.

We grabbed our orders and then headed toward a booth in the back corner.

"This stuff is awesome!" Danielle said, taking a huge gulp of her milk.

"No kidding," I said. "What do you think, Olek?"

We all looked at Olek, but he couldn't even talk because he was basically inhaling his milk. He had a huge grin on his face as he drank. We laughed.

"That good?" Dillon said.

"Is like liquid treasures!" Olek said.

That was a pretty fitting description, I had to admit. This was a pretty nice addition to the town. I mean, maybe things wouldn't end up being so boring here after all? First I find out that there's a top secret government agency in my town that I get to be a part of. Then I find out there's this cool new milk bar in town. And, I made a new friend who couldn't be more funny and interesting. My boring North Dakota routine was taking an insanely cool detour.

"I will miss this place when I go back home!" Olek said.

"We can come back tomorrow," I said.

"No, Carson, I think he means when he goes back

home to his own country," Danielle said.

"Yes, precisely," Olek said.

"Wait, but you're not . . ." I started.

And then it hit me. Of course Olek wasn't going to stay here forever. It was so obvious but somehow it hadn't dawned on me until that moment. He was just here under witness protection until his parents could testify at that trial. Which was just three days away now. And then this would all suddenly be over. Olek would be gone, back with his family. And I'd go back to my old life. The realization hit me pretty hard.

"Are you excited to go back home?" Dillon asked.

"Yes, very much. I miss my dad. But it also makes me sad, because I will miss my new friends very much."

"Oh, Olek, we'll miss you, too!" Danielle said, getting up to give him a hug. "But you're not leaving for a while, right? I mean, how long did you say your dad's contagious goat disease would last for?"

"Right, I be here for whole school year," Olek said.

I exchanged a look with him as he said this. We both knew that wasn't true. It was just his cover story. I knew better. Olek was basically only here until his parents testified and then that would likely be it. It was the first time I had thought about it, and it basically crushed me. My friendship with Olek the past few days had helped give me everything my life had been missing. Excitement, intrigue, and the chance to be a part of something big. Something important. But I realized sitting there, right then, that even more than that stuff, I was just going to miss hanging out with Olek.

"This is so good!" Dillon said, slurping the rest of his milk through the straw. "I want more!"

"Yes, me as well!" Olek said. "May we order large bucket of milk to go? I will take bath in this tonight."

I was too bummed to even laugh with the rest of them, so instead I just took another drink of milk and tried to focus on the next few days and not think about anything beyond that. If I really only had three days left with Olek, then I'd have to make the most of them.

10010110101000001010100101010100100000
)1010100100100101010010100101010100101(
1010100001001010010101010010101010101010
)0001010101010101001100101010101010101010
)101010101010000010100101010100101010100
1010100001001010010101010010101010101010
)00011001100101010101010101010
)010   0010101010100101010100
101   1010100101010101010
CHAPTER 32   10101001010101010101
             11801016101010101(
)0(

CHAPTER 32

THE NEXT DAY AT SCHOOL, THE ONLY THING ON MY MIND WAS getting either Agent Nineteen or Blue alone so I could talk to them about the phone technicians we'd seen the day before after school. They probably had seen them as well, but I thought I should tell them anyway, just in case.

I headed for the music room before first period. Nineteen was there, but so was another kid. It looked like Mr. Jensen was helping him take apart and clean his saxophone.

"Hey," I said, as I walked into the classroom, "Uh, Mr.

Jensen, can I talk to you for a minute? About the school play?"

Agent Nineteen looked at me and I could tell right away that he knew it was about Agency business.

"Can it wait? I'm busy helping Charlie with his sax."

"Not really, I have detention after school, so this is the only time I can talk," I said.

He sighed. "Sorry, Charlie. I'll be right back."

He led me back into his office and then into his real office through the secret entrance that opened when he played a jingle on the piano. It seemed like overkill to me. We could have just whispered or something.

"We can't be too careful," he said as he closed the door behind him, practically reading my mind. "So, what is it?"

I told him as quickly as I could about seeing several suspicious guys dressed as phone company technicians outside the school the day before. Then I told him about how they hadn't seemed to notice us at all.

"It was right of you to come tell me," he said. "We noticed them as well and are checking out the lead. We don't want to move too aggressively or they may suspect they're getting close. The good news is the plan seems to be working very well. We have noticed a significant reduction of Pancake Haus activity in and around the school today. We have reason to believe they're moving on to the other middle schools in town. Good work, Zero. You're doing a great job so far."

"Thanks," I said, nodding.

For the rest of the day I didn't see anything suspicious, guys in suits or phone technician uniforms or black sedans or anything of the sort. Which made sense if what Agent Nineteen had said about the plan working was true. It was sort of odd, though. The days until the ITDO trial were ticking away and things only seemed to be getting more normal as it approached. In most spy movies I'd seen, it was the opposite. Things usually escalated in some crazy way as the time ran out. Yet, for two days, Olek and I and my friends just hung out, went to movies, played games, and pretty much acted like normal kids.

Wednesday was exactly the same. We went to school, went to class, went to detention. Nothing suspicious at all.

After detention, Zack, Ethan, Danielle, and Dillon caught up with Olek and me and asked if we wanted to play basketball on the outdoor school court.

I didn't particularly love basketball, but Ethan and

Zack were obsessed with pretty much all sports and they talked Dillon, Danielle, and me into playing with them from time to time. I figured what better way to make Olek look like a normal American kid with nothing to hide than to hang out and play a normal American sport?

"What is object of game?" Olek asked as we all stood there, picking sides.

Zack groaned. It had just been decided that it would be me, Zack, and Olek versus Dillon, Danielle, and Ethan. Zack was really competitive, so I'm sure finding out that one of his team members didn't even know how to play was the worst thing that could happen to him at that moment.

"You just try to score on the other team," Zack said.

"How I make score?" Olek asked.

Zack let out a small growl and dribbled the basketball really hard a few times.

"You need to get this ball through that hoop," he said.

"Put this ball through this hoop?" Olek asked with a skeptical look on his face. "This makes no sense. It is not possible."

Zack slapped his palm to his forehead. "Can we change teams?" he asked.

"Come on, let's just play," I said.

Zack whined for a few more minutes but eventually relented and we started a game. And after just a few minutes, he seemed resolved to take every shot himself. He only passed it to me whenever absolutely necessary, and never to Olek.

On our fifth or sixth time down the court, Zack got triple-teamed and dumped the ball off to me. Two of the defenders quickly switched back to me, leaving us all covered, except for Olek, who was standing in the corner behind the three-point line all by himself. I didn't want to embarrass him, but I also thought Zack would kill me if I turned the ball over. And Olek was the only one of us who was open.

Olek held out his hands, asking for the ball.

I passed it to him, hoping he would at least be able to catch it. He caught the ball with ease and then before anyone could hardly even react, he sent up a shot that tore through the net with that satisfying *swish*.

Zack threw up his arms and yelled, "Nice three, Olek!"

Olek grinned at me and then pointed at the other team as they all gaped at him.

"Yes, I make it snow storm here," he said. "Is a bad blizzard."

"You made it rain, Olek," I corrected him.

248

"Yes, this what I say," he said, still smirking.

We finished the game, now with Zack and Olek basically owning the court, seeing as how I'm an average player at best. Our team ended up winning four out of the five games we played. Olek almost never missed a shot.

"So, maybe I'm crazy," Zack said as we all sat around, cooling off before heading home. "But I think you've heard of basketball before."

Olek laughed. "Yes, there are many players in NBA from countries near mine, like Mirza Teletovic, Toni Kukoc, Zydrunas Ilgauskas, Andrei Kirilenko, Vlade Divac, Darko Milicic, and my favorite player, Viacheslav Kravtsov."

"Wow," Zack said.

"Yes," Olek said with a nod.

We were all too surprised to say much else. It was pretty awesome to be able to give him something he probably would never get to experience here otherwise. Which was just a fun game of basketball with friends. Real friends. He must have been really lonely before, just hanging out alone at his old safe house all the time. I was pretty sure that nobody at my school besides my friends knew how funny he was.

But having so much fun that day after school just reminded me again that it was all going to end soon. The ITDO trial was tomorrow night. I didn't know what to make of it, but I did know that it was getting harder and harder not to think about how it would all be ending soon. And once it did, I had a feeling that North Dakota would feel even emptier and smaller to me than it ever had before.

CHAPTER 33

Later that night, I found myself unable to sleep. It wasn't just the hard floor I was sleeping on because I'd let Olek have my bed. No, it was the same thing that had been bothering me all week. It was the realization that this would all end soon. The trial was tomorrow night and my mission of integrating Olek had worked like a charm. Nobody had seen anything suspicious since Monday after school when we saw those guys in maintenance uniforms snooping around the school.

I should have been happy. I mean, here I was succeeding so well with my Agency mission that the enemy wasn't even looking anywhere near our school anymore. I'd basically saved Olek and, in a way, the whole country.

Plus, I'd gotten to help out real-life secret agents. I'd gotten to be a part of something important, something significant. So I should have been happier than I ever was before. But I wasn't. I realized I was being selfish, but I just didn't want it to end. I didn't want things to go back to the way they were before. I didn't want to lose my new friend. I couldn't help feeling that way, even though I knew better. I knew I should be happy that Olek would get to go back to his family soon because of me.

But instead I was sad because we only had less than two days left together.

"Olek?" I whispered. "Are you awake?"

"Yes," he said.

"Do you mess up all those sayings on purpose? To be funny?"

He rolled over in the bed and looked down at me like he had no idea what I was even asking him.

"What you mean? My English is near flawless execution."

I smiled. "Never mind," I said. "It doesn't matter either way."

"If question does not matter, then why ask?" he said.

"Yeah, good point," I said.

"Let me ask *you* question," Olek said.

"Yeah, go," I said.

"What makes you want to be agent?"

"Well . . . it was partly because I wanted to help you," I said.

"Me? But you were with Agency before me, yes?"

"No, you're my first assignment. But that's not the only reason. I also wanted to because I hate it here. This town is so boring. Nothing ever happens. And no matter what I do, I'll just end up like everyone else, stuck in some boring job with no chance to get out."

Olek was silent for a while. I wasn't sure if he understood what I was talking about. Or maybe I'd offended him, complaining about being here when he was the one with real problems. I must have sounded like a jerk.

"I mean, I know you have it harder than me," I added. "I shouldn't complain."

"No," Olek said. "No, you can say this. I know how you feel. This is why I am stuck here away from my family also. In my country, things are always the same, too. My parents try to change things there, and look what happen to them. They try to make things better and now we are apart, and I am here. But I like it here. I like this town. To me it does not seem boring. To me, this place is weird and interesting. Example: Remember when I find perfectly good boot in street?"

I laughed quietly. "Yeah, I remember."

I realized he was right. It was all about perspective in a way. His family had done exactly what I'd been trying to do my whole life. Of course, they had done so in a real, meaningful way. That was the difference. All I ever did was put on stupid pranks. They had risked their lives to make a difference. That's why North Dakota felt so much bigger to me now. Because now my stupid pranks, like getting Olek detention, actually were making a difference in a bigger way. Which only brought me right back to the harsh reality that pretty soon I'd have to go back to meaningless pranks that would only make things seem better in the short term. Good for cheap laughs and nothing more.

"I know I'm probably not supposed to ask this, but what's your real name?" I said.

"To pronounce correct I need to cut out your tongue," he said.

"Seriously?"

"Of course not," he said with a grin, but then said nothing else.

"So, are you going to tell me your real name?" I finally asked.

He leaned back in the bed and seemed to think it over. Then he shook his head.

"You're my friend," he said. "Olek is my name to you. Whatever name I had does not matter anymore. That old name is no more. This is my home right now; Olek is my name while I stay here, the name that my new friend already calls me."

"We are real friends now, aren't we? We're not just fake friends for the good of your cover?"

"Yes, Olek and Carson are like vinegar and cabbage," he said, holding his first two fingers together.

"Vinegar and cabbage?"

"Yes, is good combination, no? Is best meal. Number one tasty mixture."

"In America, we would say we're like salt and pepper, or peanut butter and jelly."

"Peanut butter and jelly?" he said incredulously. "This make no sense."

I was pretty sure all countries had heard of peanut butter and jelly, but maybe not. Or maybe he was just messing with me again. But it didn't matter. Because either way, the sting of knowing that in two days I likely wouldn't get to hear his jokes anymore washed out everything. So I didn't say anything else. Instead, I just lay there on the floor and tried to remind myself that I should be happy that I was saving my friend and the country.

CHAPTER 34

SOMETIME IN THE MIDDLE OF THE NIGHT, I BECAME AWARE OF someone shaking me. Hard. In fact, I was being shaken so hard, I was getting a headache. At first I thought I was dreaming that I was inside a blender, getting pureed into a Medlock Custom Milk flavor. But I quickly realized the shaking part was not a dream.

"Carson!" someone whispered.

I opened my eyes and saw Olek's terrified face peering down at me. He shook me again and I sat up.

"What's wrong?" I whispered.

"Somebody is inside house," he said.

"It's probably just my brother. He stays out late a lot," I said, and started to lay back down.

"No," Olek said. "He come home two hours ago. I hear it. It's them, Carson."

The stairs creaked. The third stair always creaked. I glanced at my alarm clock. It was 3:36 a.m. Olek was right—someone was in our house and coming downstairs. My room was the only one in the basement other than the laundry room and the den. There was no reason for anyone in my family to be coming down here at three in the morning unless my mom had developed a sleep-laundry habit.

My first thought was that it couldn't possibly be the Pancake Haus. For one, how would they have even found out he was here in the first place? And two, how did they get past the Agency protection that I'd been told would be stationed around my house 24–7 while Olek was here?

But then I looked at Olek's terrified face again. And I knew his instincts were right: this couldn't be a good thing. I didn't know what was going on, but I knew that I was the only one who could do something about it.

I shot out of bed and crawled over to my closet. I

opened the duffel bag containing all of my secret-agent gadgets and grabbed my Agency transponder. I didn't think about anything. All I did was act. I pressed the red emergency button for ten seconds, then put the bag on my bed and climbed on top of my desk so I could reach the basement window near the ceiling in my room. It was a pretty small window, but I thought Olek might be able to squeeze through it.

"Olek, I'm going out to the hallway to investigate. If they get past me, go out the window and run, okay? Don't look back."

He nodded.

I clicked the window latch open and pushed. It swung open slightly. I peeked outside and saw a pair of black combat boots just a few feet away. They shuffled and turned toward the window. I closed it and climbed back down off my desk.

"Never mind," I said. "Can't go that way. Stay right behind me. We'll have to fight our way out."

He swallowed and nodded. I thought for a second that he might puke and I wouldn't have blamed him. I thought I might puke myself.

But there wasn't time to think about barfing. I grabbed the smokescreen tool and strapped it on my wrist. Then I put in the night-vision contact lenses. I heard a soft shuffle from the den just outside my room. They were close now. I grabbed the tranquilizer pen and stuck it into the pocket of my flannel pajama pants.

The bedroom door was slightly ajar. I eased it open with my finger and peeked into the hallway. The night vision contact lenses worked amazingly well—it was almost as if every light in the house was on. The hallway was still empty, but I could feel the presence of at least one enemy agent lurking out in the den, just out of view.

My heart was in my throat. Maybe Agents Nineteen and Blue would get here before I actually had to do anything? But I couldn't bank on that; I shouldn't even have been hoping for it. If these guys had gotten past the Agency protection outside, then they likely would be ready for any reinforcements that arrived.

While shuffling back into my room, I debated what to do. Basically all I had going for me was the element of surprise. They likely still didn't know that I knew that they were in the house. I had to somehow use that to my advantage.

I motioned for Olek to follow me and then quickly crawled out of my bedroom and to my left, away from the den. I moved as quickly as I could while trying not to make a noise.

We crept into the laundry room adjacent to my bedroom. I poked my head out the door and saw an empty den. Maybe they weren't in the house after all? Maybe we'd both imagined hearing the noises? But how did that explain the dude with army boots just outside my window?

Then I saw someone in a ski mask and black fatigues crouched behind the couch. He was turned away from me and making hand signals to someone behind him. In his hand was a machine gun.

I ducked back into the laundry room. I scooted to a position where I could see my bedroom door without having to extend any part of my head past the laundry room doorframe. I would wait until they moved inside my room, then I'd make my move.

Olek was shaking beside me. He wasn't crying or anything; he was just shivering slightly. From fear or from being cold, it didn't matter either way. The fear was there regardless, I knew that. Even if he wasn't scared, I was scared enough for both of us.

How did they know Olek was here? Maybe Agent Nineteen or Agent Blue had been compromised and they'd forced it out of one of them? That thought made me sick to my stomach, so I pushed it out of my head. Knowing how this had happened wouldn't help us, anyway. I just needed to focus on the problem itself.

Then the enemy operatives made their move. Before I even realized what was happening, two of them rushed inside my bedroom. A third strode past, heading right for the laundry room.

He saw me just a second too late. I hadn't even remembered taking the pen from my pocket but somehow it was already in my hand. I lunged forward just as he reached the doorway and pointed the gun at my face.

I jabbed the pen into his leg at the same time I clicked out the needle. I quickly clicked it again. The gun clattered loudly to the floor a second before the unconscious body thumped down on top of it. There was no way the other intruders hadn't heard that.

For a moment, I debated going for the machine gun the guy had dropped. The problem was that I honestly would have no idea how to use it. I'd never actually held a real gun before. In North Dakota almost everyone hunted, but for whatever reason my dad never took it up as a leisure activity. So I was one of the few kids in the state who had never been hunting, and thus didn't know how to use a gun. Not only that, but I wasn't sure I'd actually be able to point it at a real, live person and pull the trigger, anyway.

But I knew I had to act quickly either way since the first of the two intruders who'd entered my room was now in the hallway. I backed into the laundry room and quickly reloaded the pen the way Agent Chum Bucket had instructed me. I turned to Olek.

"I'm going to distract them," I whispered, "you just get out of here, okay? Run right past us and get outside and then run and hide somewhere. Nineteen and Blue are hopefully on the way."

He started shaking his head, but we didn't have time to argue about it. I turned away from him and fired three discs from the smokescreen gun strapped to my wrist. I aimed them at the hallway, at an angle so that they'd ricochet toward my room as they went off.

It worked and I heard a surprised cry from the hallway as it filled with smoke. The fire alarms did not go off, which made sense. The chemical fog must have been treated not to set them off.

But it didn't matter. I grabbed Olek and pulled him into the hallway. It was too foggy for me to see anything at all, even with my night-vision contacts in, but this was my house and I knew it better than Olek knew Jimmy Buffett songs. As soon as we exited, I turned left and put my back against the wall, pulling Olek with me.

A few seconds later, a black combat boot landed inches from my leg. I swung the pen toward where the calf attached to the foot. It connected with something, and I clicked the toxin releaser.

The guy fell unconscious to the ground right in front of me.

Then I jumped to my feet and ran with my elbow out in front of me toward the den, bracing for impact. I was definitely much smaller than the third intruder, but he couldn't see a thing and had no idea I was coming. So the force of my elbow running full speed into whatever part of him I hit sent him reeling backward with a grunt.

"Go, run!" I yelled. "Back door!"

There was a brief separation in the fog as Olek passed us. Through the edge of the fog, I could just see a pair of legs scrambling up the stairs at the far end of the basement den. Olek had made it out of the basement at least. I just had to hope there were no other enemy operatives outside other than the guy I'd seen standing by my bedroom window. Or that he'd be able to make it past them somehow.

I got up to follow Olek out, but a hand that must have been made of steel grabbed my ankle and pulled me backward. Then there was suddenly a knee pressing down onto my neck and cheek. It felt like the top of my head might just explode all over the carpet like a zit.

I tried to call out but I could barely even breathe, let alone make a noise. My vision started going black and then I heard a crack. Suddenly the pressure was gone and I saw the guy falling over.

My brother Austin stood over me, looking down with a baseball bat in his hand.

"Carson, what's going on?" he asked.

Before I could even open my mouth to reply, a hand came up behind him. A hand holding a syringe. It plunged into my brother's neck. His eyes rolled into the back of his head. A pair of arms emerged from the fog and caught my brother and gently laid his unconscious body on the floor.

"Zero, where is Olek?" a familiar voice said.

I sat up and saw that the guy with the syringe was Agent Nineteen. He rushed forward and dropped to a knee next to the assailant my brother had hit with the bat. He also stuck him with a syringe. Then he turned back to me. The smoke was clearing and his face was calm, except for his fierce and wide eyes, which cast about the shadows of the basement urgently.

"Can you hear me, Zero?" he said. "Where is Olek?"

My voice wouldn't work for some reason. So I just shook my head with my useless mouth hanging open. I took a deep breath and tried again.

"I don't know. He ran, I think out the back door," I said.

"Wait here," he said and leaped up the stairs in what seemed like three steps.

With my back to the wall, I sat up fully. My brother was slumped over next to me, still breathing. Why had Agent Nineteen done that? I didn't really even have time to consider it further because just thirty or forty seconds after Nineteen had left, Agent Blue came downstairs.

"Zero," he said, kneeling next to me, "are you okay?"

I nodded.

"Good."

"What did you guys do to my brother?" I asked.

"Don't worry, he'll be fine. Are there more agents? I need to know!" his voice was short.

"There are two more, down there," I said, pointing toward the hallway.

Blue leaned over both unconscious enemy operatives for a few moments. It was hard to tell from where I was sitting, but I was pretty sure he'd injected them each with something.

"Carson? Carson, what is going on?" It was a panicked voice at the bottom of the stairs.

My mom. Then she saw my unconscious brother and the strange guy with a machine gun lying next to me.

"Oh, Austin!" she yelled and ran over to my brother. She knelt over him and touched his forehead. "What happened?"

Agent Blue walked over to her and put a calm hand on her back. Before she or I could say anything more, with impossible and smooth quickness, he had a syringe in her neck and was pressing the plunger down. Like my brother, she slumped forward, unconscious in under a second.

"What did you just do to her?" I nearly yelled, climbing to my feet. I seemed to finally be snapping out of whatever kind of daze I'd been in.

"Is there anyone else home?" he asked, instead of answering my question.

"Why would I tell you? So you can go inject them with some strange drug?"

"Is there anyone else home, Zero? We don't have time to argue!"

His eyes beamed so intensely that it almost looked like they were on fire.

"I won't say until you tell me what that is," I said.

"This is just a mild tranquilizer," he said. "They'll wake back up in a few hours. It's for their own protection."

"No, no one else is home," I said. "My dad is away on a business trip."

"Come on, we need to get your brother and mother back to their beds," he said.

I helped him carry my mom and brother upstairs. We didn't talk during either trip. Then he took out another syringe from a small black duffel bag in our entryway.

"What's that?" I asked.

"Remember that drug we gave to the janitor? This is the same thing. It will make sure they won't remember any of this."

"I don't know. . . ," I started.

"It's safe. Or, safer than them knowing what happened here tonight. It's in the interests of national security that no one in your family remembers this."

I nodded and then he went down the hall to their rooms. When he came back, he motioned for me to follow him back downstairs.

"Help me get these guys to our van," he said, motioning toward the enemy agents.

"Is Agent Nineteen out looking for Olek?" I asked as we picked up the first one.

Blue held the guy under the armpits and I had his legs. He was much heavier than my mom and brother had been.

"Yes, he is," he answered.

"You'll be able to track Olek somehow, right?"

"Don't worry about that right now, just help me," he said as we started up the stairs.

I didn't say anything else as we hauled all three of the unconscious enemy agents to a black van parked in the alley behind my house. There was already a fourth guy in the back, which I assumed had been the guy I saw on my lawn when I'd looked out my bedroom window. After we finished getting the last guy in the van, I finally decided to ask the questions that had been bothering me since the attack began.

"How did they get past the agents supposedly watching my house? And how did they know Olek was here? What happened? I thought the plan was working." I rattled off the questions so fast that I had to take a few deep breaths when I finished.

Agent Blue turned and looked at me for a few seconds. Then he started toward the driver side of the van.

"Wait, aren't you going to answer me?" I said, trailing him.

"Just stay put and wait for instructions," he finally said.

"But . . ."

"Zero," he said. "Stay here and wait for instructions."

Then he got into the van and drove away. I stood there and watched the red taillights until they had turned the corner at the end of the alley. Then I went back inside my house. It didn't feel much like my house anymore.

I cleaned up downstairs to try and make it look as if nothing had gone on. Then I went to the dining room and sat at the table. How had this happened? How could Pancake Haus, or whoever those guys were, have found out Olek was here?

$\mathbf{A}$T SOME POINT I MUST HAVE FALLEN ASLEEP AT THE TABLE because before I knew it I was being woken up by my mom.

"Carson, are you okay? What are you doing up here?" she asked.

I sat up and looked around. It was morning. She was already dressed and ready to leave for work.

"Sorry, I couldn't sleep and came up to get a snack. . . . I must have dozed off," I said.

"Well, you and Olek are going to be late for the bus.

You better go get him up and get ready," she said.

"Yeah, totally," I said, and then hurried downstairs.

It wasn't until I was in the shower that I realized that neither Nineteen nor Blue had come back during the night to give me any sort of instructions. Or tell me if they'd found Olek.

So I just went to school like normal. I didn't know what else to do. At every stop on the bus ride, I kept hoping Olek would get on. But he didn't. And I suddenly had a very bad feeling that he maybe hadn't gotten away after all.

It was more than I could take. I hated even simple jobs like mowing the lawn or taking out the trash, so why had I ever agreed to take on a real adult job, one that related to things as important as other people's safety and national security? The Pancake Haus had still gotten to Olek, probably, and I hadn't been able to stop them.

Olek was not at school that day. And as the day wore on, I realized I was more worried about Olek than anything else. I no longer cared that I'd failed. I didn't even care about the terrorists going free or the Agency failing to do its job. I just wanted to know that Olek was okay.

"Hey, I have to tell you something important," Dillon said at lunch.

"Not now, I had a rough night," I said. Understatement of the year.

"It's *really* important," he said.

I seriously doubted it would be more important than what I'd been going through since the night before, but at the same time maybe it would be nice to have one of his ridiculous theories distract me for a few minutes. So I was just about to tell Dillon to go ahead and tell me whatever he needed to when I found the message in my pizza, underneath the rubbery layer of cheese.

I quickly palmed it and put my hand under the table before peeking at the message:

Meet us by the track immediately.

"What's wrong?" Danielle asked. "You look like you're gonna blow chunks."

"Yeah, I don't feel too well," I said. "I gotta go, guys, sorry."

"But . . ." Dillon started.

"I promise we'll talk later," I said, before basically running to the trash can to empty my tray.

Both Agents Nineteen and Blue were at the track waiting for me. Neither of them smiled as I approached, and I knew right then that the worst was true: Olek had not been found.

I was barely able to keep walking. But somehow I made it over to them.

"Zero," Nineteen started, "nice work last night. You performed very well in a tough situation."

I nodded, unable to say anything. I wished they would just say it, get it over with quickly, like ripping off a Band-Aid. Then Agent Blue did just that.

"Olek has been captured."

"How can you be so sure? He might just be hiding," I said.

"Because the Pancake Haus has released evidence that they have him," Agent Nineteen said. "To notify interested bidders. The good news is that we know he is still alive for now, Zero. And we're going to do everything we can to get him back."

"How do you know he's still alive?" I asked hopefully.

"Because the ITDO trial is scheduled for this evening," Agent Nineteen said. "He's no good to them dead. They released video footage time-stamped this morning, in which he was still alive and well. They need to use him as leverage to stop his parents from testifying, so we have until tonight to find where they are holding him. We have one possible lead, and we will explore it to its fullest extent."

"What's the lead?" I asked.

They looked at each other for a moment, exchanging one of those looks that told me what was coming next before they even had to say it.

"We can't tell you that," Agent Nineteen said. "Because the fact of the matter is that we . . ."

"We're letting you go, Carson," Agent Blue said flatly.

I thought I detected a certain emphasis on my name. As if by saying Carson instead of Zero, he was driving the point home.

"What?" I asked.

"Olek has been compromised," Agent Blue said. "They know who he is now, and so your prime directive is no longer part of the mission. We can take it from here. Please don't blame yourself."

"I'm sorry," Agent Nineteen said. "You did a good job, but ultimately there's nothing more you can do. We will contact you to collect any Agency-issued equipment within a few days."

I nodded. There was clearly no point in arguing.

"Did you find out how they knew? I mean, I thought the plan was working," I said.

"We did, too," Agent Blue said, shaking his head. But he offered nothing further.

"We need to go," Agent Nineteen said. "Consider yourself relieved of duty, Carson."

Then they turned and started jogging toward Swallow Nest Hill without answering my question. I assumed that they simply didn't know and were maybe too embarrassed to say so. But either way, it wouldn't have changed the facts:

1. Olek had been captured.
2. I had failed.
3. There was nothing I could do to fix this.

CHAPTER 36

DILLON AND DANIELLE WERE WAITING FOR ME BY MY LOCKER after detention that day.

"Hey guys," I said, trying my best to act as normal as possible.

"I need to tell you something," Dillon said breathlessly.

"I still think he's nuts, but I have to admit I've never seen him so worked up about anything before," Danielle said.

"Okay," I said, not really caring either way. "Let's hear it then."

"The circus!" Dillon said almost before I'd even finished. "The circus, it's, they're . . . evil!"

"Everyone knows that," I said. "They abuse all the animals and make like forty clowns live in one small trailer together."

"It's not just that," he practically shouted. "They're a front. I mean, the circus is a front for some terrorist cell or evil spy organization of some kind. And they're planning something huge here in town. I just know they're bent on world domination."

"What makes you think all of that?" I asked.

"Because, I just know," he said. "It all adds up. Remember a few weeks ago when I told you I saw a spy dressed as a lion tamer snooping around the water treatment plant?"

"Yeah, so?" I said. "Seeing a lion tamer creeping around doesn't mean that the circus is the front to an evil terrorist cell."

"But it's not just that!" he said. "Hear me out. Then, there was the bearded lady I saw with a duffel bag of machine guns outside the Burger King near my house. Remember? Plus, I've noticed all these guys creeping around the school lately. At first they were wearing business suits, but then earlier this week a bunch of them were wearing maintenance uniforms of some kind."

I nodded. I did remember him mentioning seeing a bearded lady with guns outside of Burger King. Plus, he was right about the guys hanging around the school because I'd seen them, too.

"What do the guys in uniforms have to do with the circus, though?" I asked.

"Well, at first I thought they were posing as phone-company dudes. But then I realized why their uniforms looked so familiar to me. They're the same ones that the janitors and ride-maintenance guys always wear at the circus every year! They're unmistakable because they all have the same patch on them. The one with that MCMC logo on it. The same logo on the circus tickets the past few years."

"MCMC is the phone company, Dillon. It stands for Minnow Communications Management Company, remember?" I said.

"I know, but that's just a coincidence. The phone company might be MCMC technically, but they actually go by just MCC and their logo is way different. Look."

He held out a piece of paper. He'd printed a picture of

the phone company logo. Next to that was a photocopy of a circus ticket. And next to that was a grainy photo of one of the maintenance guys who'd been around our school earlier that week. And he was right, the logo on the uniform was from the circus, not the phone company.

"And there's more," he said. "That day of the goat prank I saw two guys abducting another guy on the corner of Sixteenth and Burdick. I saw it from the goat trailer after I released them."

I knew he wasn't making that up, because I'd seen it, too. I realized that Dillon would have had a perfect view of that from where his cousin had parked the goat trailer in an alley across from the school.

"How does that connect to the circus?" I asked, remembering that the guys had creepy white faces.

"Well, the two guys had painted white faces," Dillon said. "Which at first didn't make sense to me. But then after I remembered the lion-tamer guy and added up all these other things, I realized that their painted faces fit right in."

I tried to swallow, but my throat didn't seem to be working anymore.

"Like clowns," I said.

Dillon grinned and then nodded. "Like clowns," he agreed.

He was right. Pancake Haus had been operating under the guise of the local circus all along. The very thing that I had come to see as the epitome of a boring North Dakotan existence had been the key to everything the whole time. Then I remembered Agent Nineteen telling me that they knew Pancake Haus had been operating in the area for at least a few weeks. Right around the same time the circus came to town. And this weekend was their last one before moving out, conveniently right after the ITDO trial scheduled for tonight.

It all fit together perfectly.

"You believe me this time, right?" Dillon said hopefully.

"How would you guys like to go to the circus right now?" I asked.

The biggest smile I'd ever seen spread across Dillon's face. It was probably the first time I'd ever agreed to investigate one of his theories with him.

"Are you nuts?" Danielle said. "You can't possibly be serious! Don't encourage him."

"I think he might be right this time," I said.

"What? Why? Just because some guys wearing

uniforms with the circus management company's logo on it were at the school one day? That doesn't mean anything!"

"Maybe not, but maybe it does," I said. "You can't know for sure either."

Dillon looked too happy to even be capable of speaking. I don't think he'd ever heard someone else defending a theory of his before. I could only imagine how awesome that must have felt.

"So, are you coming with us or not?" Dillon asked her.

Danielle sighed. "Okay, fine."

She even let a grin sneak onto her face. As much as she got fed up with Dillon's theories, she still loved a good mystery and fun shenanigans as much as we did. Even if she thought it was all made up.

Except that I knew that this time it wasn't made-up shenanigans.

We rode the school bus to my house so I could get a few things that I thought might come in handy. Then we would head toward the city fairgrounds, where the circus was held every year.

When we got to my place, the first thing I did was find my Agency transponder and press the red button. The problem was that I had no idea when they'd respond.

I didn't even know if they were still paying attention to my transponder. Should I wait there for them to contact me and explain what was going on, or just head toward the circus on my own?

As I debated this, I grabbed my backpack full of gadgets and then went to the bathroom to reload and strap the smokescreen gun to my wrist so Dillon and Danielle wouldn't see it. I reloaded the tranquilizer pen and also strapped on the false palms. After all, there was really no point in holding back.

By the time I was ready to go, there was still no sign of any Agency personnel. But it was already almost five o'clock. There just wasn't time to wait any longer. I'd have to do this on my own. The ITDO trial was just a few hours away now. I might already be too late as it was.

Besides, Agency participation might only look suspicious and tip off the Pancake Haus if Olek was actually being held somewhere on the fairgrounds. It was likely incredibly irresponsible of me to put my friends in danger like this, but at the same time what could possibly be more unlikely than a kid secret agent? Well, besides a monkey secret agent that is? The answer is three kid secret agents. Having Dillon and Danielle with me instead of trained agents might be the only thing that would help keep my cover as we looked around. I'd be able to infiltrate the circus much better without the Agency. This was my fault, my problem, and my choice. I was going to make it right again.

So we hopped on our bikes and headed out, just the three of us. I rode my bike, and Dillon and Danielle shared Olek's bike.

Once there, we paid the admission at the circus main gates and went inside. The circus in our town was more like a circus–fair hybrid. There was still a giant tent where there were shows every four hours on the weekends consisting of elephants and trapeze artists and all that stuff. But there was also a whole other section with a few carnival games and rides and a freak show and a fun house.

"So where do you suppose the actual headquarters for this evil organization is at?" I asked once we were inside.

"It's in a small gray building behind the fun house," Dillon said.

"Are you sure?" I asked.

He nodded as if I'd asked the most obvious question possible.

"How do you know that?"

"Because I saw suspicious-looking guys going in and

out of that building when I came here to investigate last week."

"You came out here investigating last week?"

"What? You think that just because you never come with me that I don't still check things out? The world doesn't revolve around you, you know? I don't need your approval to believe in my theories."

His words stung, but only because they were so true. Was I really all that great of a friend to Dillon? I mean, hadn't I really just been using him for my own enjoyment all these years? I realized how selfish I'd been all this time, never truly considering that he actually took his theories seriously. And it hurt even worse now that I was starting to realize he'd probably been right about more of them than I ever would have guessed.

"You're right. But I'm here now, and I believe you. So how do we get into this building?"

"The only way to get in is through a secret entrance in the fun house mirror room," he said.

"How could you possibly know that?" I asked.

"Pfft," he said. "Because I know. It's kind of obvious, if you think about it."

I didn't know how that made any sense, but as usual with Dillon it was best to not try to make sense of the way his mind worked. Besides, after how badly his words a second ago had cut through me with their brutally sharp honesty, I wasn't about to start arguing with him about his theories again. At least not so soon.

"But that's definitely the headquarters?" I asked.

"Yeah, I know it is," Dillon said.

"Well, let's go, then."

"Is this really such a good idea, guys?" Danielle spoke up.

She had come along because I imagine she thought this all might be kind of fun. But now she looked really worried, as if there was a chance she thought Dillon might be right as well. Because if he was right, then she'd know like I did that this was no game.

"Isn't this kind of dangerous? I mean, what are you planning to do if we do break in and you're right?" she added.

"We'll take them down, of course," I said.

Which was sort of true, but really my primary directive was what it had been from the beginning: to find Olek and keep him safe. That's all I was really focused on at the moment.

Dillon nodded, and so, with a sigh, Danielle relented. We all headed to the fun house. Once we got to the hall of mirrors, we stopped and Dillon looked at me.

"Well?" I said.

He looked unsure of himself for the first time. Then he started inspecting the various mirrors, his distorted concentration reflected all around me. I watched him with interest, wondering if this was really going to go anywhere.

There *was* a nondescript gray building behind the fun house. We'd all seen it as we approached. So he was right about that, at least. But it looked to me like it was probably just a maintenance or utility building. The only thing that kept me from abandoning the plan was my pure desperation to save Olek.

"It should be here somewhere," he muttered.

"You don't really know if there's a secret entrance, do you?" I asked, too anxious to keep waiting.

He sighed and shook his head. "No, but I really do think that building is where all the evil plots go down, because of what I saw the first time I came here."

Danielle nodded. "You know, I came with him that time, and even I have to admit, now that I think back, there was something kind of sinister about the guys going in and out of the building that day. I didn't want to admit it to myself, but . . ."

That sealed it. Danielle had never once agreed with her brother. It must be the right building. Which meant we had to find a way in.

"Wait," I said. "If you saw them come out, then that means the building has its own door?"

"Well, yeah, duh," Dillon said. "I just assumed it was locked and that there had to be a secret entrance somewhere."

I rolled my eyes, and wanted to laugh even in spite of the situation. But I didn't. I couldn't even smile until I found Olek, let alone laugh. Time was ticking away. I kept forcing myself not to think about the possibility that it might already be too late. And also the scary fact that I'd pressed the red button on my transponder almost an hour ago and still hadn't heard from the Agency at all. What did that mean? I forced myself to forget all that. Now was a time for action.

"Come on, let's go," I said.

We left the fun house and circled around to the back. There was a chain-link fence that blocked us from actually getting to the building behind the fun house. I mean, we could easily climb it, but there were several guys milling around near the building's front entrance.

They would definitely hear and see three kids climbing the fence.

Not only that, but then there was the problem of how to get past those guys and into the building even if they didn't catch us climbing the fence. And suddenly I realized that I shouldn't be thinking in terms of "we" anymore. There was no way I could let Dillon and Danielle come inside with me. Not with how dangerous I knew this would be.

"We need to create a diversion of some kind," I said. "So I can get in there."

"Why are you getting so gung-ho about this?" Danielle asked.

"Because, what if Dillon were actually right for once? I mean, we need to stop these guys!" I said. "I'll check it out, but I still need your help."

"Why don't we just call the cops?" Danielle said.

"No way!" Dillon said. "The cops are in on it!"

"I agree with Dillon," I said.

"What?!" Danielle said.

"I mean, not about the cops being in on it, but do you really want to call the cops with no proof whatsoever? What do we tell them, that our crazy friend has this theory that the circus is a front to an evil organization with aspirations of world domination? They won't even hesitate before hanging up on us, let alone send out any uniforms to investigate."

"Good point," Danielle ceded. "Plus, this will be more fun, right?"

That was the thing about good pranksters. We all knew how to put aside danger for the excitement of creating mayhem. Of course, now the mayhem actually served a purpose. So it was more of a distraction than a prank.

"The question is, how do we create a diversion big enough to get all of these guys away from the building?" I asked.

We all pondered this for a bit. An elephant roared somewhere in the distance behind us. Then Danielle smiled.

"I got it!" she said. "Remember a few weeks ago? The goats? Nothing can clear an area better than herds of animals."

01100101101010100000101010010101010010000
.0101010010010010101010010100101010100101
)1010100001001010010101010010101010101010
)00001010101010101001100101010101010101010
)0101010101010000101001010100101010101010
)1010100001001010010101001010101010101010
)00001010101010100110010101010101010101
.001010110101000100101010101010101010101
)101010000100101001011010101010101010101

CHAPTER 37

WE WENT BACK TO THE MAIN CIRCUS TENT AND THEN WALKED around behind it. There was a high fence running out of the sides. The fence was lined with green tarp, but through a few holes, I could see rows of animal cages and trailers. Some large and some small. But I didn't even need to see it, because I could definitely smell it. There were also some trailers for people as well, which I assumed were for some of the performers.

On Thursday they only did one main circus show at night, which didn't start for at least an hour. That was likely about as good as we could ask for since it meant there probably weren't too many performers back there getting ready yet.

We followed the fence back to the far corner. The only other things in that area were a few port-a-potties, an old maintenance shed, and a bunch of garbage bags waiting for pickup.

"Do we just climb it?" Dillon asked, looking up at the top of the high fence. It was at least nine feet tall.

"I'm going to climb it," I said. "You guys head back to the fence's gate and wait there. Once I'm in, I'll come let you in and then we can get to work."

They nodded and helped boost me up to the top of the fence. I dropped down on the other side. It was a lot higher than I figured, because when I landed, my ankle rolled. I grabbed it and curled up, doing everything in my power not to yell out in pain.

"Carson, are you okay?" Danielle whispered from the other side.

"Yeah, I'm fine. Go," I whispered back.

I looked around. There were no people in sight at the moment. There were, however, two cages containing several huge tigers. They stood, like statues, and stared at me with a look of hungry curiosity.

I also saw a few massive pens that I could only guess must house the elephants.

Then I heard a voice. I crawled desperately behind a large garbage can that was clearly used for animal poop, trying not to gag as I crouched among the spill off. I covered my nose with my shirt, but it didn't help.

"Hey, Tigress, what's up?" the voice said. "What do you see? Huh? What about you, Dan, you see something, too?"

Who names one tiger Tigress and the other one Dan? But I pushed the question aside, because it didn't matter right then. I peeked out from behind the trash can and saw a guy wearing jeans and a flannel shirt standing by the tiger cages.

There was a giant ring of keys looped to his belt. It was like a gift from the circus gods. I said my thanks and then tested my ankle. It was sore and already swelling, but I had so much adrenaline pumping through my body that I barely felt any pain. Although I knew that by tonight it would be impossible to even walk on it.

I dug out the tranquilizer pen from my bag as quietly as possible and then crawled out from behind the poop can and worked my way toward the trainer. He was facing away from me. I readied the pen. The tigers saw me and tensed.

"What's the matter?" the trainer asked them again as if he actually expected an answer.

I was six feet away now and one of the tigers started making a low, guttural, and menacing noise. It wasn't really a growl so much as it was a promise to eat me. The trainer, realizing something had caught their attention, whirled around.

"Hey" is all he managed to say before I jabbed the pen into his thigh and released the toxin. He stumbled back and slumped against one of the tiger cages.

The tiger started toward him. I saw where this was going and didn't like it. I hurried over and grabbed his shirt and pulled him away before the tiger could turn him into dinner. I wasn't strong enough to drag him, but I was able to get him to slump forward, just out of the tiger's reach.

I reached down and unhooked his huge key ring. I'd been planning to let out all the animals, but upon seeing the tigers' hungry faces up close, I decided that might not be the smartest thing to do. So instead, I stayed low and made my way over to the fence's gate.

After trying a dozen keys, I found the one that opened the lock. Dillon and Danielle were waiting outside just like we planned. I handed her the key ring.

"I'm going to make my way back over to the building," I said. "The window of opportunity to sneak in might be small, even with this big of a diversion, so someone should be there, ready to get in."

"You're gonna go in alone?" Dillon asked.

"No sense in all of us risking it," I said. "One person can sneak in way easier than three."

"He's got a point," Danielle said.

"After you let out the elephants and horses and all of the non-carnivorous animals, just run. Head to the bike rack out by the front entrance and lie low. If I don't meet you back there in one hour, then get on the bikes and take off."

"What's going on?" asked Dillon. "You know more about this than you said, don't you?"

Normally, this kind of accusation from Dillon would be met with eye-rolling and groans. But this time, he was right.

"Look, I can't explain everything right now," I said. "But . . . I think Olek might be in trouble. He told me once that he had gotten into some trouble with the circus. At the time, I had no idea what he meant, but now it all makes sense. He went missing last night, and I think he's here somewhere. Promise me that if I don't show up in an hour, you'll just get out of here."

Dillon and Danielle gaped at me with blank stares.

"Please say you'll follow those instructions," I said. "Please!"

They both nodded slowly in unison. It was rare moments like this when I remembered that they were twins.

"Good. Thank you. Now go let loose some animals. Let's wreak some havoc on this place."

They nodded again and started toward the elephant pens as I turned to exit through the open gate. But then Danielle called out to me.

"Wait, Carson," she said.

I turned back.

"Good luck," she said. "And please be careful."

"You, too," I said back.

For the first time in history, we would be pulling a prank together and likely not have a whole lot of fun doing so. But at the same time, I had to admit that it was too bad we weren't at school; this would have been the greatest prank in school history. The look on Gomez's face alone would have been worth the likely expulsion.

CHAPTER 38

THE SCREAMING STARTED JUST A FEW MINUTES AFTER I'D
exited through the gate. By that time I was already halfway back to the fun house, even with my swollen and
stiff ankle. I stopped to rest it for a second and looked
behind me.

There were animals everywhere. Some were calmly
sitting around, eating grass. But others were wreaking
havoc. One elephant had already tipped over a small food
stand. Monkeys were bouncing around and screeching
and throwing stuff. It was pretty awesome. I just hoped

nobody ended up getting hurt.

As I got back to the fun house, I saw men in uniforms and employees running by me, heading toward the growing chaos without even giving me a second glance. I was as good as invisible among the growing crowd of people running away from the circus tent and the few employees running toward it.

By the time I'd used the key grappling hook to scale the fence separating the fairgrounds from the gray building and lower myself slowly down the other side, the area was nearly deserted. I ducked behind some Dumpsters just across from the building. I only saw one door, and it appeared to have an electronic lock. Which meant that some sort of keycard would be needed to get inside.

I dug the Agency transponder from my bag and pressed the red button again. Then I hid it under the Dumpster. If I got captured, I didn't want the enemy to find it. But I still had some hope that the Agency would eventually respond and that it would lead them here.

As I crouched there and watched the building, I reloaded my tranquilizer pen. At one point the door opened and some guy dressed as a clown came rushing out. Probably an armed clown. He dashed off toward the circus tent. I guessed with a mess this big they needed as much help as possible.

After he ran off, I sprinted as fast as I could with my bad ankle across the pavement toward the building and put my back to the wall right outside the door, behind the hinges, so the door would hide me from view when it opened again. I figured I wouldn't have to wait long. Even from here, I could see a huge elephant charging across the fairgrounds, a massive banner dragging behind him.

A few minutes later, a guy wearing a security shirt came bursting out and started toward the big tent area. He didn't even make it three steps before I'd jammed the pen into his back. After he fell, I grabbed his security card and used it to enter the gray building. Once inside, it took me a moment to remember to breathe. My heart pounded so hard in my chest, I felt like I might start choking on it.

After taking a few deep breaths to calm myself, I realized I was looking down a long, brightly lit hallway, not unlike the hallways at my school. But I didn't waste any more time taking it all in.

I fired several smokescreens into the hallway. In a matter of seconds the whole place was clouded in a gray haze. I stayed low and against the wall as I worked my way from door to door, coming out of my crouch only long enough to look inside the window on each door.

Most of the rooms were empty. I imagined most of the employees were out trying to help contain animals. The circus was a good front for an enemy spy cell in that nobody would ever suspect it. Well, nobody except for Dillon. But its one major flaw was that there was a lot that came with running a circus.

As the smoke started dissipating, I fired several more smokescreens down the hallway in front of me. So far, I had yet to see another person in the building, but it was better safe than sorry. After maybe twenty rooms and two full hallways, I finally found what I was looking for.

I knew it as soon as I saw it. It was a door without a window. The only one I'd come across so far. I held up the keycard to the reader, but the light on the lock stayed red. I tried it again and this time it beeped at me but still didn't open.

So I reached into my pocket and took out a fruit roll-up. After unwrapping it, I stuffed it inside the door frame by the lock. The soft gooey fruit roll-up explosive squeezed in pretty nicely. Then I found the paper detonator. I moved down the hall a few feet and pressed down on the microchip.

There was a muffled bang and then the faint smell of

burning metal. I crawled back over to the door and saw that the electronic lock was blown to pieces. The door swung open slowly on its hinges.

Inside was a short hallway with four other window-less doors. I checked the first two and found an office with a cluttered desk and a smaller room with a small cot and a gross-looking toilet. The fourth room was just like the second room, but the main difference was that it was occupied.

"Olek!" I said.

"Carson, no," is what he said back.

He was alive! I couldn't believe I'd found him.

Olek looked mostly unharmed. But the panic on his face told me everything I needed to know: It was a trap.

I turned around and found myself face-to-face with Mule Medlock's easy smile.

"Hello, Carson," he said, and before I could even respond, everything went black.

CHAPTER 39

I OPENED MY EYES TO A BLURRY HAZE. THE FIRST THING I FELT was my throbbing ankle. The next thing I noticed was that I couldn't move my legs or arms. Then I heard a voice.

"It's good to see you awake." It was Mule Medlock's voice. "You're much more useful this way. The funniest part is that you really believed you'd be able to sneak in here completely unnoticed and rescue your friend."

I tried to talk but all that came out was a mumble.

"Don't strain yourself, Carson. We have time. It's still amusing to think that the Agency actually employed a kid. That's a new low, even for them. It's immoral and unethical on so many levels. Anyway, here, have some milk."

Suddenly a cup was pressed against my lips and milk was poured. I was still groggy so most of it ended up on my shirt, but I did manage a few swallows. I couldn't place my finger on the flavor, but it was good. Even in this dire situation, I noticed that much.

"Like it?" Medlock said. "It's a dragon fruit and watermelon four-and-two-thirds percent blend."

Finally, my eyes began focusing. We were in a fairly large room. I saw no tables or any other furniture. It was just a bare, bright room with only one door that I could see. But Olek was also there, sitting in a chair a few feet away from me. He appeared to be unconscious.

His head was slumped forward and he was tied to the chair with what appeared to be heavy duty bungee cords across his torso. I found that I was as well. My feet were held to the chair legs by white plastic zip ties. My shoes were no longer on my feet, and my left ankle was bleeding through my sock. That one must have been injured when they'd knocked me out. My hands were tightly bound together behind me by what felt like the same type of plastic zip ties.

Mule Medlock stood in front of me. One guard in a suit stood behind him. A little person stood across the room, between Olek and me. Not, like, a small person, but, you know, a really small person. A little person. According to my social studies teacher, they're not supposed to be called midgets. I was guessing this one doubled as a circus performer for his cover, which seemed kind of mean to me, but then again no one was forcing him to be part of this evil organization, or the circus.

The little person held a large, leather black bag in one hand. He smiled at me.

I glared back.

"That's my friend Packard," Mule said. "Packard is going to have some questions for you later. And I'm sure you'll comply, since he tends to get answers when he really wants them."

Packard put his bag on the floor and started removing items from it. He took out a lot of metal gadgets that looked like they were from a horror movie. My stomach lurched, and I puked up the milk I just drank all over my shirt.

"Eww," Medlock said, taking a step back.

"What do you want? Why are you doing this?" I asked. "I don't understand why you want to hurt people."

"Me? You think I want to hurt people?" Medlock asked.

"Why else would you be trying to help known terrorists?"

"Power, of course. Why else? Hurting people and gaining power are not mutually dependent endeavors. One can be achieved without the other. If people get hurt, that's unfortunate. But sometimes necessary."

"But how does keeping these terrorists out of prison help you get power?" I asked.

"Well, the money is a good start," he said with a smile. "Certain associates of these alleged terrorists are paying us a pretty hefty sum to stop Olek's parents from testifying. In fact, his parents know we have Olek and have already agreed to back out of the trial. What they don't know is that they'll still never get Olek back. We've agreed to sell him to one of these terrorist groups. As for what they plan to do with him, that's really none of my concern, nor is it any of my business.

"But none of that stuff really matters, anyway," he continued with a dismissive wave of his hand. "What matters to me most is what will be perceived to be an epic failure on the part of the Agency. It will be the largest and most public failure in its history. It will destroy them from within."

"So you're doing all this just to take down the Agency?" I asked. It seemed like a completely ridiculous motivation to me.

"Yes! And with them out of the way, there will be nothing to stop a new authority from rising up. We'll restore meaning back to this country, and I will be there to oversee it all. I'll be a hero, a god of sorts. The man who saved America from itself."

"But acts of terrorism and sabotage won't convince anyone that you ought to be in charge," I said.

"No? Tell me then, how can we change a system that has been locked in place for decades? How can we change the unchangeable? People in this country are stuck. They are stuck and they don't even know it. They get up, eat food, go to work at a job they don't truly love to make money to buy stuff to try and fill the voids. They've all been stuck in the same routine for generations and they're just begging to be broken free, whether they know it or not. The first part of that is simply to destroy the institutions holding them hostage, metaphorically speaking of course."

I shook my head. I heard what he was saying but didn't want to believe him. It was just too close to what I'd been telling myself about North Dakota my whole life. I wasn't anything like Mule Medlock, was I? I've always wanted to break free from what I'd always perceived to be a boring prison of routine, but not at the expense of others. Besides, for me it had always been North Dakota specifically. Surely things were different, more exciting, bigger and better for kids in other places, right? There was no way a kid in New York City or Hawaii or Tokyo felt as bored and trapped in as mundane an existence as I did.

Right?

"What's the matter?" he asked. "Are you realizing that I might be right?"

"Whether you are or aren't, you can't hurt innocent people to make your point!" I said.

"Why not?"

I didn't answer him.

"No, seriously," he said. "I want you to give me a specific reason why a few people getting hurt for the greater good is wrong. Go on. Tell me."

"Because . . . because it's just not right," I said,

frustrated that I couldn't come up with anything better than that.

He just laughed. But he didn't laugh like a normal, sane person. No, he was practically having a seizure he was laughing so maniacally. He was acting like some crazed villain straight out of a bad James Bond movie. And I had to face the possibility that Medlock might just be plain crazy.

"You're insane," I said quietly once he had calmed enough to hear me.

"So? What's your point?" he asked.

I clenched my fist and suddenly felt a small poke. My false palms. They hadn't found them. I started slowly working the razor blade free, concentrating on moving my shoulders as little as possible.

"Anyway, let's start by you telling me who your Agency contacts at the school are, shall we?" Mule Medlock asked.

"I don't know what you're talking about."

"We both know that's a lie."

"It's not."

I'd finally managed to free the razor with my first two fingers. It was clutched delicately between them. The trick now would be to get it to my thumb without dropping it or cutting myself.

"No matter. I will get you to talk eventually. Or, Packard will, anyway, to be more accurate. You'll be willing to tell me your darkest secrets, your most embarrassing dreams by the time he's done with you. I promise you that."

"Well, being that I'm dead anyway, can you at least tell me how?" I asked. "How did you know? I mean, how did you find out who Olek was? And that he was at my house?"

I finally managed to get the razor gripped between my first finger and thumb. The problem was that I couldn't seem to bend my wrist the right way to get the razor to the plastic thing holding my wrists together.

"It was you," Medlock said. "You told me everything I needed to know."

"I don't—" I mumbled. "I don't understand."

"Well, that's what being a troublemaker gets you," he said. "I targeted you due to your inability to stay out of trouble. It seems you have a certain nose for it. I knew that the Agency headquarters was located here in town and thus they'd likely bring Olek here as well, assuming it to be the safest location. But, of course, we still didn't know who he was. All of you middle school kids look the same. So that's where you came in."

"You mean . . ." I started, but trailed off, still trying to process what he was implying.

"That's right, it was all staged. That wasn't really Agent Orange, and that wasn't really his PEDD. Or it was; we just made some alterations. Agent Orange was captured well before that handoff. I had a feeling that if I had my agents follow you after we gave you the box, it would eventually lead us to Olek. And sure enough, just a few days later, you're suddenly hanging out with this new kid."

"So you've had people watching me this whole time? Ever since the day I got the package?"

He nodded, his eyes glowing.

"If you knew all along, why did you wait so long to make your move?" I asked.

"Why not?" he said. "By waiting until the last day before the trial, it gives the Agency almost no chance of recovering Olek in time. That's also why we had our men back off from your school and your neighborhood, to make the Agency think their plan was working. To get them to let down their guard ever so slightly."

I shook my head. No, it couldn't be. The idea that I had been indirectly responsible for Olek's capture was more than I could bear. I kept shaking my head, trying to make the facts go away. Trying to make them untrue.

"It's true," Medlock said.

And I knew he was right. It explained why I hadn't been able to identify Agent Orange in that photo lineup Blue and Nineteen had shown me. If only I hadn't been so selfish, so stupid, so eager to believe I could become a secret agent, then his plan wouldn't have worked. Had I just delivered the package to Mr. Jensen, never opened it myself, Olek would probably still be safe.

"How?" I said. "How could you have been so sure I'd open the package?"

Medlock laughed.

"Are you kidding? Look at you. Of course you're going to open it. You're obviously desperate for attention, with all the pranks and whatnot. Letting loose herds of goats? Of course that kid will open a mysterious package! You know, you remind me a lot of myself when I was a kid. Always dreaming of bigger and better things. Well, pretty soon you're going to realize that genuinely bigger and better things simply don't exist in this country. At least not in its current form."

Was I really that predictable? I didn't need to think about it for much more than a second to realize that the answer was obviously yes.

Just then a small metal cart with wheels was brought in, and Packard began loading his tools onto it. He hummed lightly while he worked. I think it was a song from a really old Disney movie, but I couldn't be sure.

"But that still doesn't explain how you found out that the Agency had a base here, or that they'd bring Olek here," I said.

"Well, some things must remain a mystery. Sorry, Carson. I can't give away all my secrets. You know what the difference is between people who are good at what they do and those who aren't?"

I shook my head. Not that I really cared either way at this point.

"Attention to detail," he said. "That's it, that's the secret to success. That's why my milk is so good: I *pay attention to detail.*"

I groaned and shook my head. But really I did that to cover up what almost became a shout of triumph. I'd finally found a way to position my wrists so the razor made contact with the zip tie. I slowly began working it back and forth. I couldn't press hard enough to cut it easily, but with enough finagling, it would give eventually. Or so I had to hope.

That's when Olek woke up. He rolled his head groggily to the side. When he saw me, he smiled faintly.

"I see we are both in a jar of vinegar-soaked cucumber," he said to me.

"We're in a pickle, Olek," I corrected him.

"Yes, this what I say," he said.

"Ah, good, we're all awake," Medlock said. "So we all get to witness what happens next. I'm going to turn the floor over to Packard now. Like I said, he has some questions for you, Carson."

Medlock took a few steps back and stood next to the guard. He smiled and watched the little guy push the metal cart over to the space right in between Olek and me.

Packard picked up a nasty-looking pair of pliers. They were like normal pliers, except they had what looked like human teeth affixed to the end.

"Did you know that the human bite can be among the most painful things a person can experience?" Packard asked. "When people get attacked by sharks they often don't feel any pain at first, only pressure. This is because sharks' teeth are so sharp that they just slice through flesh with little resistance. Human teeth, however, particularly the incisors and bicuspids, are just sharp enough to break skin with enough pressure, but dull enough to cause maximum pain."

He walked over and stood in front of Olek. The truth smacked me right in the face: they weren't actually going to torture me; they were going to torture Olek. And they wouldn't stop until I told them what they wanted to know.

CHAPTER 40

"**W**AIT," I SAID, "YOU CAN'T DO THIS!"

Medlock laughed. "Oh, but we're not doing this. You are. We will stop as soon as you tell us what we want to know."

"I will. What do you want to know?" I said, knowing that I was being weak. But I didn't care; I couldn't sit there and watch them torture Olek.

But I also kept working the razor back and forth. I was starting to make some progress now. I was maybe one fifth of the way through the thick plastic tie. I worked faster, knowing that I was already so panicked it would simply look like my shoulders were trembling from fear rather than working to cut myself free.

"How many contacts at the Agency did you have?" Packard asked.

"I . . . I don't know," I stammered. "I only communicated with them via email."

"You're lying," Medlock said.

"No, I swear!"

Medlock looked at me and then nodded at Packard. Packard grabbed a chunk of Olek's arm with the teeth pliers and started applying pressure. Olek's scream was about enough to destroy me.

"Okay, okay!" I said. Packard released the pressure slightly.

"Carson, no, don't tell," Olek yelled.

"Just one. There was only one guy."

Mule Medlock studied me. Then he shook his head. "I'm disappointed that you clearly care about your friend so little. Packard, proceed."

Packard once again squeezed the giant teeth pliers and then started twisting. Olek screamed so loud that my will just shattered. I know this makes me a horrible secret agent. But I couldn't handle knowing that I was causing Olek so much pain.

"Three! I only had contact with three guys at the Agency. I swear that's the truth this time!" I shouted, referring to Agents Nineteen, Blue, and Chum Bucket.

Packard released Olek's arm. I saw that the skin where he'd gripped him was already purple and blue from bruising. Blood dribbled down where several teeth had broken the skin. Olek didn't cry, though; he just breathed deeply and rapidly.

"There we go! See?" Medlock said. "We already knew that, of course, since we've been following you from the day you got the package, remember? But thank you for finally telling the truth."

"If you knew that, then why did you ask?" I shouted. I kept working the razor. I was close to halfway now.

"Just to see how far we had to push to get the truth out of you," he said. "Not very far at all, I must say. See? This is one of the problems with hiring a kid to do secret-agent fieldwork. You just break so easily. You have no willpower, no discipline. Well, at least not enough to be an Agency operative. But their mistake is my gain, as usual."

He nodded at Packard to continue. Packard looked at me and grinned.

"Tell me the names of your contacts?" he said. "Both their codenames and covers."

"I really don't know! They never told me!" I shouted.

Medlock shook his head and Packard gripped one of Olek's thumbs with the teeth pliers. He squeezed and started twisting it. I heard a snap as Olek's thumb broke. He screamed so loud it was almost deafening. Then Packard moved on to the other one.

At the same moment I was finally able to cut through the zip tie. The guard and Medlock were both watching Packard do his thing and didn't see that I was loose. I reached down and quickly sliced the ties on my ankles and then lifted my elbows, allowing the bungee cords to slide up my arms and round my neck.

Mule Medlock looked at me with pure shock right as I emptied my smokescreen gun into his face. Then I lunged at him, screaming as pain ripped through my ankles. My shoulder connected with his midsection as smoke billowed around us.

He fell backward into the guard who had already drawn his pistol. They both fell to the ground as he fired several wild shots. I heard pings of ricocheted bullets in the confined space.

I rolled off Medlock. I could no longer see due to the

smoke, but my hands found the guard's face and I jabbed both my thumbs into his eye sockets. I pushed so hard I thought I might kill him. He screamed and flung me off him. I hit the floor pretty hard, but I knew I'd done some damage. The fog was thick, but through the haze I could see the guard flailing blindly on the ground.

Where was Mule Medlock? I spun around and saw him lying on the ground with a pool of blood blooming under him. He must have gotten hit by a ricocheting bullet. I crawled through the smoke, no longer able to put any weight on my ankles, in the direction of Olek and Packard.

Packard found me first. He came rushing out of the smoke with a giant saw in his hand. He swung it at me and I managed to just duck the blow without even thinking. I was on my knees, which put me at about an even height with him. I grabbed his whole torso in a massive bear hug, pinning his arms at his sides. Then I pushed all my weight toward him and we slammed to the hard tile floor.

Packard wheezed, the wind knocked out of him. I rolled left and then got back to my knees. He tried to get up but stumbled. I grabbed his hair and yanked back as hard as I could. He screamed and I ended up with a handful of black hair.

Hey, I know it's cheap, but right then I just wanted to win the fight. By any means necessary. Who cared if it was by cheap means? I was fighting for our lives, after all.

Packard swung his fists at me wildly, but I was able to duck away from his pretty short reach. Then I grabbed wildly at the cart of tools. My hand closed around a massive syringe. Through the smoky haze, our eyes locked.

He held up a huge white knife made from what looked like a sharpened tusk. He swung it at me so quickly that I was barely able to fall back and out of the way. I actually felt a whoosh of air hit my face as the blade sliced just past my nose.

As I fell backward, I threw the syringe. I heard a soft thump and screaming. I climbed back to my knees and saw Packard running around wildly in the fog, the giant syringe lodged in his forehead. He was so out of control in the smoky haze that he ended up running right into the concrete wall with a thud. He slumped to the ground, blood dripping from a clearly broken nose.

This was turning into a bloodbath.

"Olek, are you okay?" I called out.

"Not really," he replied calmly.

I guess it was a silly question being that he had

two broken thumbs and a nasty bite mark on his arm. Although his reply meant he was alive, which was good enough for me.

"I'll cut you free soon," I said.

"No rush," he said.

"My eyes, I can't see," I heard the guard moaning from somewhere behind me. "Kid, what did you do to my eyes?"

I crawled over to Olek and cut him free. His hands and arms were swollen and looked really painful. But he seemed to be in high spirits anyway.

"I knew you rescue me," he said. "You're best agent I ever meet."

"I don't know about that," I said, remembering that I was the one who had gotten us into this in the first place. "I can't walk, Olek."

"Here," he said. The smoke was lifting now and I saw him swipe his arm across the metal cart, shoving all the tools onto the floor. "Get on."

I climbed onto the cart. "Can you push it? With your thumbs and everything?"

"No worry, I got it," he said.

He grabbed the cart with his fingers only. His crooked thumbs dangled below his palms.

"Take us over to Packard," I said.

Olek wheeled us over to him. He was still breathing but completely knocked out. I reached into his jacket pocket and found a set of car keys with a security keycard attached to it. Just in case we encountered any locked doors while making our getaway.

"Okay, ready," I said.

Olek pushed us toward the door, past the guard who had passed out with his hands covering his eyes. I knew he wasn't dead because his chest heaved.

I used Packard's keycard and shoved the door open. Olek pushed the cart forward and suddenly we were jammed in the door frame. I gave the door another push and looked back at Olek. He grinned as he struggled to get the cart through.

Behind him I saw a pool of blood on the cement where Mule Medlock had been lying. But Medlock himself was no longer there.

0100101101010000010101001010100100000
0101010010010010101001010010101010101
1010100001001010010101010010101010101
0000101010101010010110010101010101010
0101010101010000010100101010010101010
1010100001001010010101001010101010101
00001010101010100110   101010
00101011010100010010   1100
1010100001001010010   1010

CHAPTER 41

"**O**H, CRAP, OLEK, WE HAVE TO GO, NOW!"

Then I saw Medlock. He stumbled toward us, one hand over his stomach where he'd been shot, the other holding a gun. He fired just as Olek gave a final push and freed us from the door frame.

"Are you hit?" I asked.

"Like Beatles song?" he asked.

"Not now," I shouted, even though I knew his answer was as good as a no. "Let's go!"

The cart moved pretty quickly down the hallway with

Olek running while pushing it. Mule Medlock was running behind us, or more stumbling than running. But he was firing. Bullets whizzed past us, sometimes slamming into the wall just ahead of me. Had he not had a bullet wound in his stomach, I was pretty sure his aim would have been more deadly.

When we were finally at the outside door, Olek stopped the cart and ran around to open it. He grabbed the underside of the cart and pulled us both outside. The cart hit the doorframe and tipped, and we both spilled onto the pavement as the door swung closed. I sat up and Olek struggled to get to his feet with his injured hands.

Men with machine guns ran toward us from across the huge lot. Medlock must have hit some kind of alert. Then I saw the Mini Cooper. Its custom license plate read: PACKARD.

I locked eyes with Olek; he must have been thinking the same thing. We both nodded as I started crawling toward the car. The approaching men began firing. A few bullets hit the side of the car, and I heard them shouting.

"Don't hit the dark-haired one. We need him alive!"

The shooting stopped, but they were getting close now. I used the keys I had taken from Packard to unlock the car. We climbed inside. I sat in the driver's seat. I'd never driven before but figured it couldn't be too hard. I'd seen my mom do it thousands of times. I started the ignition and put my foot on the brake, then yelled out in pain.

"Olek, you have to drive. I can't use the pedals!" I yelled.

"I can't steer," he said, holding up his mangled thumbs.

"Uh, okay, you work the pedals, I can handle steering," I said. "Press the brake."

He crouched on the floor and then reached over and pushed on the brake pedal with his knuckles, wincing as he did so. I shifted the gear stick to *R*, which I assumed meant reverse.

"Okay, gas!" I yelled.

He slammed his hand onto the gas pedal and the car's tires screeched and then suddenly we were zooming backward, way faster than I expected. Through the rearview mirror, I saw the men with guns diving out of the way.

I turned the wheel. "Brake!"

Olek hit the brake, and the car started spinning as it slowed. We must have spun at least 720 degrees before finally stopping. I smelled burned rubber. I quickly surveyed the road ahead. We were now facing the fence that separated the gray building from the main carnival area. I looked behind me. There were seven men with machine guns climbing to their feet.

"Gas, punch it hard!" I shouted.

Olek did, and after spinning for a second, the tires got their grip and we fired forward like a rocket. I screamed and held the wheel as steady as I could as we slammed into the fence. The car crashed right through it. We raced straight toward a ticket booth.

"Less gas!" I shouted.

Olek let up, and I spun the wheel. I turned it way too far, having no idea what I was doing. The car spun again, and I felt the right wheels lift up as we almost tipped over. Then we skidded to a stop, just missing the ticket booth.

"Gas!" I said as I saw the men chasing us on foot through the rearview mirror.

The fairgrounds looked empty. They must have closed it after the animal debacle. It was dark outside now. I looked down and found a switch with a drawing of a light on it. I pulled it out and the headlights switched on.

"Okay, easy gas," I said.

And then we were driving. It was a jerky, bumpy, swerving ride. But we managed to find the park entrance. The gate was closed. It was one of those dual metal triangle poles, but it looked a lot sturdier than the fence had been. I wasn't sure if this small car could break through it. I looked back and saw several dark sedans zooming toward us.

I heard more shots and then suddenly our car spun out of control and crashed into the main ticket booth, rear end first. Airbags exploded everywhere around us even though we hadn't hit it that hard.

"They must have shot our tire out," I said.

Olek climbed back up into the passenger seat. He had been thrown into the back of the car by the collision. He sat down and nodded, looking dazed. Several sedans approached quickly.

"It's over," I said. "I'm sorry. I tried."

"Is okay," he said, and sighed.

Then a car pulled up on the other side of the front gate. The door opened, and Agent Blue got out of the driver side. He jumped the front gate and ran over to our smashed car, pulling out a pistol.

He pointed the gun at the approaching black sedans and fired four shots. All three cars spun out of control as their tires were hit. One of them actually flipped and started rolling, before coming to a stop upside down.

Agent Blue opened the door to the Mini Cooper.

"What are you waiting for? Let's go," he said.

"I can't walk," I said.

He reached in and lifted me out of the car easily, flung me over his shoulder, and we all ran back toward his car. Meanwhile, another car pulled up and Agent Nineteen and two other guys I didn't recognize got out.

"I'll get them back. You go take care of the enemy operatives," Agent Blue said.

"Gray building behind the fun house!" I shouted as they hopped the gate and ran toward the crashed black sedans.

Agent Nineteen threw back a thumbs-up to let me know he'd heard me.

Then the three of us were in Agent Blue's car, heading toward the school. I wanted to talk on the way back, but I was too exhausted to do much of anything but sit there and wonder what in the heck had taken them so long.

0100101101010000010101001010100100000
0101010010010010101001010010101010010I
1010100001001010010101010010101010101010
0000101010101010100110010101010101010101I
0101010101010000101001010100101010101010I
1010100001001010010101010010101010101010
0000101010101010100110010101010
0010101101010001001010
10101000010010100101

CHAPTER 42

I THOUGHT WE WERE DRIVING TO THE SCHOOL, BUT THAT WASN'T entirely correct. We did go to the school parking lot, but when we got out of the car, Agent Blue led us away from the school. Toward the sledding hill. It was pretty embarrassing, but he had to carry me, piggyback style, since I couldn't walk on my ankles.

As we walked, he handed me a cell phone.

"Call your mom. Let her know you're at a friend's house and will be home later tonight," Agent Blue said.

I called home and told my mom I was at Olek's house,

that they were finally getting to move back in. She sounded happy for him, but I thought I detected a trace of sadness in her voice.

"Can I also call my friends?" I asked Agent Blue after I'd disconnected. "To let them know I'm okay?"

"Sure," Agent Blue said as we descended the sledding hill.

So I called Danielle and before letting her ask too many questions I simply told her I was okay and home safely and would explain more the next day. Then I hung up before she could say much more than "okay."

We went all the way down the sledding hill and around the base of it, right up to the exposed dirt hillside filled with tiny swallow nests. A small shed sat in a nearby grove of trees. A small building that I'd seen a thousand times before but never paid much attention to. I mean, it was a maintenance shed. What was there to notice about it, really?

Agent Blue opened the shed's door with an electronic keycard.

"You mean all those winter days that we've been sledding down this hill, we've been sledding right near a top secret government agency entrance all along?" I asked.

"Yes," Agent Blue said.

"But isn't that kind of crazy? To put a secret entrance just a few hundred feet from where dozens of kids go sledding?"

"You all stay away from this shed, don't you?" Agent Blue asked.

It was true. We all did. There was just something about it that made us stay away.

"We do," I admitted.

"That's not a coincidence," he said. "You ever heard of an EMF?"

I shook my head.

"It means electromagnetic field. It's a magnetic field that sometimes occurs naturally or around large metallic objects. Anyway, the theory is that really strong EMFs make people feel uneasy. So we've generated a very strong EMF within a hundred-foot radius of this shed."

"Won't our brains be fried?" I asked.

He shook his head as we stepped inside the shed.

"No, EMFs have no detectable permanent physical effects on humans."

I nodded and glanced back outside at swallow nest hill and noticed that many of the nests faced the front of the shed.

"There are cameras in those holes, aren't there?" I

asked, remembering Dillon's claim.

"They're extremely tiny and partially buried. How could you know that?" Agent Blue asked.

I debated telling him about my crazy (or not so crazy, apparently) friend Dillon's theories but thought better of it.

"Lucky guess," I said.

The inside of the shed wasn't empty like I'd expected. It wasn't very large, but it still contained everything you'd have expected it to if you didn't know it was really a secret entrance to a government facility. There was a lawnmower, some gardening tools, a fuse box, a generator, stuff like that.

Agent Blue used a key to unlock and lift up the face of an old first-aid box on the wall. Underneath it was what looked like the normal contents of a first-aid box. But then he felt around inside and pulled open a false front to reveal a small digital pad. He placed his index finger on it and then leaned his face close to the box.

A red line of light passed over his eye, and the pad under his finger blinked green. An elevator-size square panel in the floor slid open. The platform beneath it was about a foot below the floor of the shed.

Agent Blue and Olek stepped onto the platform, with

me still on Agent Blue's back.

"Keep your arms at your sides unless you want to lose them," Agent Blue said to us.

Then suddenly we were moving down, the panel above us closed, and everything went black. We were in a more normal-looking elevator now. The keypad inside had only three buttons, all of them unmarked. But they were all a different color. Red, blue, yellow. Agent Blue put his finger over the yellow button. It lit up and blinked a few times.

"You might feel your ears pop a little bit," he said.

Before I could even respond, the floor just dropped out on us. At least that's what it felt like. The elevator zoomed downward so quickly that it felt like my stomach and face were still located miles above the rest of me. As he'd warned, I felt my ears popping, just like they did when I dived to the bottom of a ten-foot-deep swimming pool.

We must have zoomed down at an incredible rate for close to twenty or thirty seconds. I couldn't believe that we were actually that far underground. We must have been close to a mile beneath the surface. Then, mercifully, the elevator finally slowed to a stop.

"How far down are we?" I asked.

"As far as is absolutely possible without putting the structure in danger," Agent Blue said.

The elevator doors opened, and I was looking at a small entryway of sorts. It was basically a little room with marble floors and several other sets of elevator doors. But straight ahead of me, through a set of glass doors, there was a huge room, bustling with people. We exited the elevator. Agent Blue used a keycard to open the glass doors and we entered the massive atrium.

"Welcome to Agency headquarters," he said.

0100101101010000010101001010100100000
0101010010010010101010010100010101010010101
1010100001001010010101010010101010101010
0000101010101010100110010101010101010101
0101010101010000010100101010100101010110
1010100001001010010101010010101010101010
0000101010101010100110010101
0010101101010001001010   0101
1010100001000101001010   0100
1010100001001010010101   010
                                  101

CHAPTER 43

THE HUGE ROOM WAS PROBABLY THE SIZE OF SEVERAL LARGE gymnasiums with high ceilings, making it feel like a cavern. It was exactly what I would have expected the main room of some top secret government agency to look like.

It had marble floors, flags, plaques all over. On the left wall there was a huge projection TV screen that took up pretty much the whole space. On the right wall there were hundreds of framed portraits of men and women. Directly ahead of me were dual glass staircases leading up to some offices with glass walls. In between the staircases was a huge American eagle sculpture flanked by an American flag and another flag I couldn't identify. Everything looked new, clean, modern, high-tech, and expensive. People crossed the room and ascended and descended the staircases in a chaos of activity.

Agent Blue saw my face and said, "We call this room the Lobby. It's the heart of the Agency. There will be time to look around later. Right now, though, we need to get you guys to the medical wing."

I was still hanging on to his shoulders as we headed left, along the wall, toward a set of metal doors in the corner of the Lobby and adjacent to several rows of glass cubicles housing metal desks and expensive-looking glass computer monitors. Most of the people working didn't even look up once as we passed.

The medical wing of the Agency HQ looked like pretty much every hospital I'd been in before. Except there were no windows and everything looked slightly more high-tech. I ended up getting a walking boot cast on one ankle, and a bandage on the other. Olek had two casts put on his hands, and his arms were secured in double slings. He looked pretty funny.

When we got back to the Lobby of the Agency HQ, Olek and I were led up the huge glass staircase overlooking everything in the atrium. Agent Blue ushered us into a conference room and before leaving told us to wait there.

Olek and I took a seat at the huge wooden table in the center of the room.

"Like striking down two chicken with one boulder," Olek said with a grin, holding up his dual casts.

"I'm not sure that metaphor really fits here, Olek," I said. "Besides, it's 'two birds with one stone.'"

"Yes, this what I say," he said. "Winner, winner, dinner of roast beef and potato."

"We'll have to work on that one, too," I said with a grin.

"What I say wrong this time?"

"Winner, winner, chicken dinner," I said.

"Ah, this make no sense!" he said. "Roast beef dinner taste much better than chicken dinner."

I didn't even bother to comment; instead I merely grinned. I would have laughed but I was honestly way too exhausted for that.

"Thank you again for coming for me," Olek said.

"You would have done the same for me."

Olek nodded. Before we could say anything else, the door opened and both Agents Nineteen and Blue entered. They sat across from Olek and me at the conference table.

"Did you get him?" I asked. "Medlock, I mean?"

"There was no one left in the building by the time we got in there," Agent Nineteen said solemnly. "This Mule Medlock guy you said was the leader must have gotten away."

"No way! How is that possible?" I said.

Agent Nineteen merely shook his head.

"We'd like you to fully debrief us, Zero," Agent Blue said.

"Uhhh . . . ," I said.

"That's just a fancy way of asking you to tell us what happened tonight," Agent Nineteen said.

So that's what I did. I told them everything, about how Pancake Haus found out who Olek was, the staging of the package delivery. When Olek heard this part of the story he seemed both shocked and maybe even a little impressed at Pancake Haus's ingenuity. I also told them how the Agent Orange I saw wasn't the real Agent Orange. How my friends and I had pieced together that there was something fishy about the circus. And I told them what Medlock had said about wanting to take down the Agency.

"He really hates you guys for some reason," I said.

"Yeah, that's in line with the little bit we've been able

to get out of the apprehended agents so far. The real question is why?" Agent Nineteen said. "And how does he know so much about us? He shouldn't even know we exist, let alone know that our headquarters is here."

"So what took you guys so long to respond to the red button?" I asked.

"We're sorry about that, Zero," Agent Nineteen said. "The whole Agency was in overdrive trying to find out what happened to Olek. All available field agents were out exploring possible leads. Since you'd been relieved of duty, your transponder's signal had actually been taken off the main grid here at HQ. It was somewhat of a fluke that Agent Blue even noticed you had sent the signal at all. After that, we got to the location as fast as we could."

"But we thank you," Agent Blue said. "You saved the mission. Without you, we would not have known Pancake Haus's location until it was too late, if we would have ever found out at all. You're a national hero."

I felt my face grow hot.

"I was just trying to fix what I'd caused," I said.

"*None* of this was your fault; we were simply duped by someone who knew more than we thought possible," Agent Nineteen said. "I just wish we knew how Medlock managed to have the drop on us the whole time. How did he know as much as he did? How did he get past the Agency encryptions in Agent Orange's PEDD to plant that trap?"

Nobody spoke for a few minutes.

They eventually debriefed me on what they'd found at the circus that night. They'd managed to apprehend eleven enemy operatives, although they found the bodies of dozens more, apparently shot by Mule Medlock to keep them from talking. Mule Medlock was not one of the people apprehended or killed in the raid.

"The little guy you said was named Packard, we didn't find him either," Agent Nineteen said.

I shook my head. "So this isn't over!"

"Zero, it's never over," Nineteen said. "Even if we had gotten Medlock, eventually another enemy would replace him. But we have dealt the Pancake Haus a major blow. It's going to take a while for them to regroup and rebuild their resources, if they ever try at all. I would say we have at least a good two or three months before we need to worry about the Pancake Haus again."

Even after all that I couldn't believe it wasn't over.

"But the important part is that we have Olek back," Agent Blue said. "And we got word of his rescue back to our operatives at the ITDO. His parents testified at the trial, and those three terrorists are as good as locked up. Forever."

"Olek will be departing to rendezvous with them again soon," Agent Nineteen said. "They can never go back to their home country, but at least they'll all get to be together as a family in our Witness Relocation Program."

"But why does he have to leave if they already testified?" I said, even though I'd known all along that he wasn't going to get to stay here.

"Because for witnesses it's never truly over," Nineteen explained. "There will always be groups of people, associates of those three terrorists, who will be looking for revenge. Though, with the trial over, they won't devote nearly as many resources to the effort. There won't be groups like the Pancake Haus after them anymore. They'll be safe in our Relocation Program."

I looked at Olek. He was smiling. Which was great, of course. I should be happy for him. But I would mostly just miss him.

"You've done some amazing work, Agent Zero," Agent Nineteen said. "Truly remarkable."

Agent Blue nodded solemnly in agreement.

And I noticed that they'd actually called me Agent

for the very first time.

"But," Agent Nineteen said.

"What's going on?" I asked.

"You're still being retired," Agent Blue answered.

"Retired?" I asked.

"It means you're free to go," Agent Blue said. "Olek was protected, his parents testified, you succeeded. Your services are no longer needed."

I nodded, surprised at both how disappointed and shocked I was that they were letting me go, despite the fact that I'd saved the day almost single-handedly.

"Tracking down and eliminating the remaining factions of the Pancake Haus isn't your problem," Agent Nineteen said. "It's ultimately too much responsibility for a thirteen-year-old. You need to be a kid, have fun, not worry about getting killed or captured for the rest of your childhood. Therefore, all records of your employment or involvement will be destroyed, and of course if you ever try to disclose any of this, it will be denied."

I nodded. "You don't have to worry about that."

I was thinking about Dillon. I realized that given everything that had happened the past week, I'd probably never consider his theories completely crazy ever again.

"I want you to know, though, that we'll always be proud to call you a fellow agent," Agent Blue said.

Agent Nineteen nodded in agreement.

"Thank you," I said, not sure what else I was supposed to say to that.

"Now, we'll leave you two alone for a moment if you want to say good-bye one last time before Olek leaves," Agent Nineteen said.

He and Agent Blue left the conference room.

I looked at Olek and suddenly found myself barely able to keep it together.

"I'm going to miss you," I said. "I wish you could stay here."

"Yes, me too, but we must go for protection. Keep hiding and stay in front of enemy. Is like game of panther and rat."

"Cat and mouse," I corrected him.

"Yes, this what I say."

"Can't you guys just stay here? I mean, this place is safe, right?" I motioned at the underground secret base we were in.

"Yes, this place like Fort Knockers," Olek said. "Very secure."

I laughed.

"But problem is this is terrible place to live. There is no sun down here. No Jimmy Buffett. No kidney bean ice cream."

"Yeah, that's a good point, Olek. But I'm going to miss this a lot. Well, at least you'll be back with your family, right?"

He smiled wider than I think I'd ever seen before.

"Yes, is good," he said.

"All right, well, bye, Olek," I said, not sure that I could stay here much longer without breaking down. "Email me or something if you're ever allowed to."

Olek nodded.

"Thank you for everything," he said. "I will not forget what you do for me. You're even cooler person than Jimmy Buffett."

I didn't think I could even say anything back without bursting into tears like a little baby. So instead of talking, I just gave him a nod and left the room.

01001011010100000101010010101010010000
010101001001001010100101001010100101
1010100001001010010101010010101010101010
00001010101010100110010101010101010101
0101010101010000101001010100010101010
1010100001001010010101001010101010101010
00001010101010100110010101010101
0010101101010001001001010101101010000100101001010010101010101010

CHAPTER 44

A SHORT TIME LATER, I WAS ESCORTED OUT BY AGENT NINE-
teen. As we approached the entrance of the Lobby, Agent
Blue called out from the top of the glass staircase.

"Agent Nineteen, I need a quick word," he said.

"Wait here," Agent Nineteen said, and then climbed
the stairs.

I wandered over to the huge wall lined with portraits
of men and women. There were hundreds of them, all
nicely framed in polished wood with small brass plates
that displayed the person's name and nothing else. Well,

their codename, that is.

There was an Agent Isotope. He was a skinny, pale guy with bulgy eyes. Then there was Agent 1100, a pretty girl who was probably only twenty-one years old or so. Agent Fuchsia was an older guy who looked like he could be someone's sweet old grandpa. Agent Brown had bad teeth and long blond hair but looked like a body builder. His neck was about as thick as my whole torso.

Agent Smiles looked like she never smiled. Agent Bloodstone looked like he probably liked to use swords instead of guns. Agent 5 would have looked almost as young as I was if it wasn't for his thick beard. And Agent Smith looked like some normal guy you wouldn't look at twice if you passed him in the street.

There were so many, I probably could have looked forever. But the odd thing was I'd yet to see one for Agent Nineteen or Agent Blue. Or Agent Chum Bucket, or anyone I recognized at all for that matter.

"There are a lot of them, right?" a voice said beside me.

I jumped and almost fell over I'd been so startled. It was Agent Nineteen.

"Where's yours?" I asked.

"I hope I won't have one hanging up here for a long, long time," he said.

"What does that mean?"

"Carson, this wall is our tribute to agents lost in the field."

It took me a few moments to really hear what he'd said.

"You mean, all of these agents are . . . dead?"

"That's right," he said. "Most of them were great agents, too. Don't feel badly for them, though. All of them had moments before they were lost when they could have turned back, given up on the mission. Maybe they'd still be alive today, maybe they wouldn't. But they all made a choice. And I think if you asked them, they wouldn't have had it any other way."

"Wow" is all I could manage to say.

"Well, are you ready to go home?" he asked.

"Yeah, I suppose," I said, taking one last look at the wall of faces. I just couldn't believe all these people were gone. I started to turn away but then stopped dead in my tracks.

"What is it?" Agent Nineteen asked.

"This guy," I said, pointing at one of the pictures,

hardly believing what I was seeing. "This guy . . . it's . . . it's . . . "

I was pointing at a picture of someone named Agent Neptune.

"It's . . . Mule Medlock," I finished.

"That's not possible," Agent Nineteen said, taking a step back. "I saw Agent Neptune die myself."

"It's him. I'm positive," I said. "I'll never forget that smile for as long as I live."

Agent Nineteen stared for a moment longer, then wiped at his eyes. It took him almost a full minute to collect himself.

"He was my partner and a close friend. He died in Indianapolis. Shot in the forehead. It just isn't possible."

Agent Nineteen was quiet for a while. Then when he spoke again, he seemed calmer. "It makes sense now—how he knows so much about the Agency. I just can't believe he's still alive. We will definitely look into this further. But that's none of your concern. We better get you home, Zero. Let's go."

CHAPTER 45

RIGHT AWAY THE NEXT MORNING, I RODE MY BIKE TO DILLON and Danielle's house.

"What the heck happened to you?" Dillon asked when he saw me limping in a walking cast. "What happened at the circus? What is going on?"

He seemed to be on the verge of a nervous breakdown. I expected Danielle to try to calm him down, to be the voice of reason like usual. But she didn't. This time, she joined him.

"Yeah?" she said. "What was that yesterday? What happened to you? Did you find Olek?"

I took a deep breath and then explained to them how I'd found out that Olek was some sort of secret agent in his home country and had gotten involved in international espionage. He'd gotten captured by the enemy spy cell operating with the circus for a front. I told them I was able to break in and save him, leaving out the parts where I'd gotten captured myself. I wanted to tell them about my involvement with the Agency, but I knew that it wouldn't be the right thing to do from the perspective of an almost sort of secret agent. It was my cover; I still shouldn't break it even though I wasn't technically working with the Agency anymore.

What I told them was all in all a pretty ridiculous story, and I'm not sure if they really believed me. Well, Dillon definitely did, but Danielle still looked pretty skeptical. But, in the end, was it really any more ridiculous than the whole truth anyway? Either way, they stopped asking questions, which was the point.

About a week later things had pretty much returned to normal. I mean, as normal as is possible when you're best friends with kids like Dillon and Danielle, and you know of the existence of a super–top secret government agency operating literally right underneath your school, that is.

And for the first time in my whole life I was sort of okay with everything being normal. I was never happier to be living out a boring North Dakota routine. And it wasn't because I'd learned my lesson or anything. I still craved action, excitement, something bigger and better than what existed on the surface. The difference now was that I actually knew better. I knew that beneath the boring and plain and predictable exterior of North Dakota life there really *was* more going on. That there were bigger things than I ever could have imagined happening right below and around us all the time. And that I had once been a part of that. And simply knowing all of that was enough to make even the most mundane North Dakota things, like going to the movies, feel anything but boring and mundane and routine.

Because even though nothing strange had happened since that night at the circus when I'd saved the day, it didn't mean I wasn't always watching. It didn't mean I wasn't always ready for anything at any time. And that's why it wasn't that shocking to me when one Wednesday I got another chunk of paper in my corned beef.

I unfolded it slowly. My hands shook, but only a little.

I looked down and read the message:

Agent Nineteen has 48 hours to live. Meet on
the school track in six minutes.

I looked up and saw Dillon staring at me.

"What's wrong?" he asked.

"Nothing," I said, grabbing my lunch tray and standing up. "I just have to go save the world again."

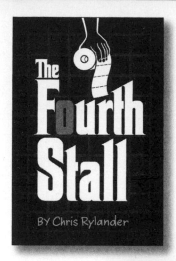